Dear Reader,

Have you ever had a secret fantasy that you've never shared with anyone? Not even your sister or your best friend? I'd forgotten mine until my editor suggested I write a TWICE FORBIDDEN book and she mentioned very casually that no one had ever written one about the ultimate forbidden fantasy—a priest.

Wow! Not only did her suggestion trigger memories of *The Thornbirds* and an even earlier movie, *The Left Hand of God,* but I remembered that long-ago summer when I was thirteen and I too had a secret crush....

When she is dumped by her swindling fiancé and becomes a person of interest to the FBI, Naomi Brightman flees to Haworth House, the hotel she runs with her sisters. But trouble follows hot on her heels in the person of Father Dane MacFarland. While he instantly rekindles memories of the teenage fantasy crush she had on a school chaplain, the raw sexual heat she feels from the moment she sees him is very real. And increasingly irresistible.

I hope you enjoy Naomi's story and my upcoming stories about her sisters, Jillian and Reese, in *Taken Beyond Temptation* (June 2010) and *Twice the Temptation* (August 2010).

Happy reading,

Cara Summers

Cara Summers

LED INTO TEMPTATION

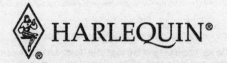

HARLEQUIN®

TORONTO • NEW YORK • LONDON
AMSTERDAM • PARIS • SYDNEY • HAMBURG
STOCKHOLM • ATHENS • TOKYO • MILAN • MADRID
PRAGUE • WARSAW • BUDAPEST • AUCKLAND

Recycling programs
for this product may
not exist in your area.

ISBN-13: 978-0-373-79544-4

LED INTO TEMPTATION

Copyright © 2010 by Carolyn Hanlon

Printed in U.S.A.

ABOUT THE AUTHOR

RITA® Award Nominee Cara Summers has written more than thirty books for Harlequin. She has won several awards, including an Award of Excellence, three Golden Quills, and two Golden Leaf Awards. She has also been honored with a Lifetime Achievement Award from *RT Book Reviews*. She loves coming up with stories for the Blaze line because it allows her to write so many different kinds of stories—from Gothic romances and mystery adventures to romantic comedies. When Cara isn't creating new stories, she teaches at Syracuse University.

Books by Cara Summers

HARLEQUIN BLAZE
188—THE DARE
192—THE FAVOR
239—WHEN SHE
    WAS BAD...
259—TWO HOT!
286—TELL ME
    YOUR SECRETS...
330—THE P.I.
336—THE COP
342—THE DEFENDER
396—A SEXY TIME OF IT
413—LIE WITH ME
437—COME TOY WITH ME
474—TWIN TEMPTATION
480—TWIN SEDUCTION
511—CHRISTMAS MALE

HARLEQUIN TEMPTATION
813—OTHERWISE ENGAGED
860—MOONSTRUCK
    IN MANHATTAN
900—SHORT, SWEET
    AND SEXY
936—FLIRTING WITH
    TEMPTATION

To my very newest daughter-in-law,
Nicole Van Markwyk Hanlon, and to my son
Brendan. I hope you bring each other a lifetime
of joy! Welcome to the family, Nicole.
I love you both!

Prologue

"TO NEW BEGINNINGS." Naomi Brightman raised her
glass of champagne and met her sisters' eyes over the
rim. It was too late for second thoughts. As the oldest
sister, the practical one, it had always been her job to
have them. Third thoughts, too. But thanks to her, the
papers were signed. She'd even drawn them up. With
enthusiasm.

From the moment she'd stepped through the front
door of Haworth House, it had exerted an odd pull on
her. For the life of her she couldn't figure it out. With
its perch on a lofty cliff overlooking the sea and the
turreted gray tower that seemed to pierce the sky, it had
conjured up images of fantasy and romance, and she'd
decided a long time ago that fantasy and reality never
mixed.

Even now, standing in the gloomy tower room that
the real estate agent had neglected to include on their
initial tour, Naomi was still convinced that this was
where she and her sisters were meant to be.

"To our first business venture," Reese said, lifting
her champagne. "It's been a long road getting here."

Naomi had been seventeen, Jillian sixteen and Reese

fifteen when they'd first hatched their plan. They'd known full well that their days together were numbered in the Catholic boarding school in the south of France where they'd been raised. Abandoned there by their father when Reese was an infant, they'd grown up inseparable. The nuns had often referred to them as the Three Musketeers. But as they'd entered their teens, it had become increasingly clear that their future career paths were going to separate them.

Jillian beamed a smile at her sisters. "To our new home."

As they all sipped their drinks, Naomi thought back to that night so long ago when they'd first toasted their dream of sharing a business venture with champagne—a bottle Jillian had snitched from the nuns' private wine cellar.

Now that dream was a budding reality. They were going to turn Haworth House, once the summer home of legendary silent film star Hattie Haworth, into a small, exclusive hotel that offered excellent food and fine decor.

Naomi's contribution had been to provide legal advice and a solid business plan. Reese, who had a growing international reputation as a chef, would handle the culinary details—design the menus and hire the kitchen staff. And Jillian, now a budding antique dealer, was going to oversee the interior design.

"Isn't it just perfect?" Jillian's voice bubbled with enthusiasm. She'd been the one who'd found Haworth House on Belle Island off the coast of Maine. It had just the kind of rich history that would appeal to her. According to Jillian, Hattie Haworth's life had been a mess when she'd retired here to the haven she'd built for herself. When the star had failed to make the transition to the talkies, her studio had dumped her, and her husband had left her for a younger woman with a more promising future.

Reese let her gaze sweep the tower room that had once been Hattie's private boudoir. "*Perfect* might be pushing it a little."

Naomi had to agree. The sunshine battling its way through the grime-coated tower windows illuminated dancing dust motes and not much else—which was probably a blessing considering the state of the faded wallpaper and the crumbling bricks in the fireplace.

Totally unruffled, Jillian said, "This tower will rehab beautifully, and you have to admit, the rest of the place is great."

"True," Reese agreed with a smile. "The kitchen has definite possibilities. And you can't beat the view." She gestured to one of the windows, where the Atlantic stretched as far as the eye could see. "But this room looks like no one has touched it in years."

"No one has," Jillian said. "I did some research in the local paper, and in the beginning—right after Hattie died—there were rumors that she haunted the place. So the new owners boarded up the tower. After that the stories seemed to fade. But none of the subsequent owners ever ventured up here."

"And you just decided to tear down the boards and barge in on a ghost?" Reese gave Naomi a rolling eye glance that said *typical.*

Jillian lifted her chin. "I think Hattie's happy to have us here."

"You think?" Naomi asked.

Jillian nodded. "The first time I came up here, I sensed her presence. Look." Setting down her glass, she grabbed her sisters' hands and drew them toward an old beveled glass mirror. "What do you see?"

"I see the Brightman sisters," Naomi said. They were so different. Jillian, with her curly blond hair, was the shortest, her style of dress early gypsy. Reese, the tallest and most striking, wore her dark hair pixie short and had on her usual uniform of jeans and T-shirt. Compared to her sisters, Naomi thought of herself as ordinary. Her hair was trapped between blond and red, her eyes a mix of green and gray. The conservative business suits and practical shoes suited her job in the Boston law firm where she worked.

"Wait for it," Jillian urged.

Seconds ticked by. They stood side by side staring into the mirror as the air chilled around them.

Jillian squeezed their hands. "Can you feel the drop in temperature?"

"You could hang meat in here." Reese's voice was hushed.

Naomi suppressed a shudder. Later, she decided that if she'd been there alone, she would have chalked it up to an overactive imagination. But when the mirror suddenly flashed as if it had caught a beam of sunlight and then shimmered, she heard all three of them catch their breath simultaneously.

For an instant, there'd been a fourth image in the dusty glass.

"Did you see her?" Jillian whispered.

"Tall, beautiful, in a filmy white dress," Reese said.

"Red-gold hair," Naomi murmured. It nearly matched

the shade of her own. And it had fallen in a tumble of curls nearly to her waist.

"And her feet didn't touch the ground," Jillian said. "Did you notice that? I did some research. Ghosts float. Their feet never touch the ground."

"Well, I'll be," Reese said.

"She's here." Jillian's tone was triumphant. "And if she didn't want us here, we wouldn't be."

For a moment there was silence in the room.

Naomi swallowed hard and wondered what had happened to her practical, sober side. She'd seen that image in the mirror. She should be telling her sisters that this wasn't going to work. They couldn't possibly live in a tower that was already occupied. But what she said was, "So we're going to build our new home in a space that's probably haunted." And as she let her gaze sweep the room again, she realized she'd made a statement, not a question.

"There's something else," Jillian said. "Something I haven't told you yet."

"What?" Naomi and Reese asked the question in unison as their eyes shot to their sister.

"There's a secret room." Jillian hurried over to the one wall that didn't have windows and pulled a lever. A panel slid open.

"Of course, it has a secret room," Naomi murmured.

"And it's just like Jillian to spring it on us," Reese said.

Even in the dim light pushing through the windows, Naomi could see that the room was small, no larger than a closet. She and Reese waited in the doorway as Jillian stepped in.

"There's more. Wait till you see." Jillian picked up a linen-covered hatbox, turned and held it for her sisters' inspection.

As she and Reese moved closer, Naomi noticed the piece of parchment fastened to the top of the box. It read:

Fantasy Box. Choose carefully. The one you draw out will come true.

Reese shot Jillian a suspicious glance. "This isn't a joke."

Jillian shook her head. "I swear it's not. I found the room the first time I came up here. I was looking into the mirror and I saw the door open behind me. But I waited for the two of you before opening the box. Naomi, you're oldest. You go first."

Naomi firmly ignored the chill working its way up her spine as she lifted the cover off. Inside were folded pieces of the same parchment as the note. Curiosity warred with a firm tug of apprehension. There had been a definite warning in that message.

She met her sisters' eyes, then carried the box to a table and set it down. "Let's all take one on a count of three. One."

"Two," Jillian said.

"Three," Reese finished.

They reached into the box and together pulled out a parchment each.

For a moment there was no sound in the tower room other than the muffled crash of waves on the rocks below.

Reese whistled softly. "I don't know about the two

of you, but the fantasy I drew out seems pretty sexual in nature."

"Me, too," Jillian said.

"I guess we know what Hattie Haworth did to amuse herself after she retired from her film career," Reese commented.

Only Naomi remained silent. She didn't think she could talk. She certainly couldn't seem to take her eyes off the words written on the parchment. What she was reading was the secret sexual fantasy that had fueled her imagination when she'd been a teenager in that French Catholic boarding school.

But who would have known about it? She'd never even shared it with her sisters. It was forbidden. Unthinkable. Yet there'd been a time in her life when she'd thought of little else. Still, there was far too much guilt associated with it.

And pleasure? A little thrill moved through Naomi as she thought of the message on the box.

The one you draw out will come true.

1

One year later...

I HAVE TO GET TO Haworth House. I have to get to Haworth House.

The words had formed an ongoing chant in Naomi's mind on the short ferry ride from the mainland and they'd become more insistent once the gray turreted tower had come into view. From the moment she'd seen it, she hadn't been able to tear her eyes away. In spite of the chill wind that had driven other passengers into the main cabin, she'd remained outside. Even now that the boat had docked and passengers were queuing up to disembark, she lingered at the railing.

Two weeks ago the life she'd built for herself in Boston had begun to unravel. First, she'd lost her fiancé and become a person of interest to the FBI. Then, two days ago, she'd been fired from her job at the law firm of King and Fairchild. The FBI thought she had something to do with the one-hundred-million-dollar-plus Ponzi scheme her ex-fiancé had been running during the six months they'd been engaged.

When she'd learned of their suspicions, she'd felt just like Humpty Dumpty after his fall—completely shattered. Every time she replayed the pivotal scenes of the past two weeks in her mind, she felt as if she were watching clips from a reality TV series. Everything seemed to have happened to someone else.

Only, they'd happened to Naomi Brightman.

But if she could just get to Haworth House, she'd figure out a way to put the pieces of her life back together. After all, Hattie Haworth had.

In the distance, a gull circled the tower, then soared into the brilliant blue sky. Little had she known a year ago when she and her sisters had toasted each other with champagne in Hattie's boudoir that her life was going to run such a close parallel to the original owner's. And Hattie had come here.

Naomi knew she was running away, something she'd never done before in her life. How could she? She'd been the oldest. It had been her job to provide a role model for her sisters. Some role model. In the space of half a month, her life had gone from girl success story to girl failure.

She simply had to get out of Boston. She needed a break from that damned prickling sensation at the back of her neck that told her she was being watched—24/7. By the FBI, the Boston police and perhaps by her ex, Michael Davenport, too. Everyone seemed convinced that her ex-fiancé was going to contact her.

The sudden sting of tears blurred her view of the tower. Blinking rapidly, she turned from the railing and bit down on her lower lip to keep it from trembling. No tears. She never cried. If it was the last thing she did, she was going to figure out how she could have been so wrong about Michael Davenport.

For a moment, she let her mind drift back to the night he'd ended things between them. He'd invited her to meet at the Four Seasons. That's where they'd first run in to each other six months ago. She'd been entertaining clients with her boss, Leo King, senior partner and her mentor at King and Fairchild.

Michael had claimed it was love at first sight for him. Had it been the same for her? She'd certainly thought so. Their romance had been a whirlwind one, and Michael was really good at the romantic side of things. There'd been flowers and little gifts, funny little trinkets that he'd given her to commemorate everything they'd done together. The Michael gifts, she'd called them. She'd kept them lined up on a shelf in her apartment.

He'd even given her one at their final meeting, a souvenir of Boston he'd picked up in the hotel gift shop. How many times had she gone over that last meeting, not only in her own mind, but also for the police and the FBI? Hundreds of times. Michael had been kind, telling her that he had to go away for a while on business. He'd lifted her hand, kissed her fingers and said he'd be in touch. All she'd read was sincerity in his eyes. And she'd believed him, just as she'd believed everything else he'd told her.

Naomi Brightman, girl super-chump.

And she wasn't sure she'd let go of him yet. In her hurry to leave her apartment without being tailed, she hadn't dared to pack a suitcase. But she'd put all of the Michael gifts in the big tote she always carried.

That made her a super-super chump.

"Is there something wrong, miss?"

Jerking around, Naomi found she had to glance up, way up, to see the face of the man who'd joined her at the railing. An instant tingle of familiarity moved through her. Why? He was tall, broad-shouldered and he wore aviator-style sunglasses that reflected back her own image. So it wasn't the eyes that made her think she might have met him before.

She quickly catalogued the dark hair escaping from beneath the hood of the sweatshirt, the strong line of his cheekbone and chin. But it was only as her gaze dropped to his mouth that the memory finally clicked.

Father Pierre Bouchard.

He reminded her of the young French priest who'd been her confidant at the boarding school where she'd been raised. No, more than her confidant, she admitted as a guilty thrill moved through her. When she'd been fourteen, she'd had a major crush on the young and handsome Father Bouchard. He'd dominated her fantasy life for over a year. And this man bore an uncanny resemblance to him.

"Do I know you?" she asked.

The lips curved a little. And Naomi felt the tingle of recognition grow even stronger. She also felt a blush rise to her cheeks.

"No. We've never met. You're sure you're all right?"

"I'm fine." She tilted her head to one side, not quite ready or willing to let it go. "You weren't ever a priest at Our Lady of Solace boarding school near Lyons?"

"Never."

It was relief she was feeling, not disappointment. He wasn't Father Bouchard. How could he be? The voice was wrong. No accent. And what were the chances of Father Bouchard ending up at Belle Island? And why in the world would she want him to? She hadn't thought of the young priest in ages. But he'd slipped into her mind frequently during the past year—ever since she and her sisters had opened up Hattie Haworth's fantasy box.

Naomi could still picture the words on the parchment paper she'd pulled out: *Your secret fantasy has always been to make love with a priest. Now you will experience all those forbidden pleasures.*

Firmly, Naomi ignored the guilty thrill that moved through her again and pushed that memory aside. She had bigger problems to solve. Straightening her shoulders, she said, "Sorry. You reminded me of someone."

"No problem."

But the feeling of familiarity lingered even as she turned and followed the last of the passengers off the ferry. Once on the pier, she couldn't prevent herself from glancing back. For a moment, their gazes locked and held. It wasn't merely familiarity she felt this time. There was also a tug deep inside of her. For an instant, she wanted to go back and talk to the stranger again.

"Hey, sugar! Over here."

Naomi snapped her head in the direction of the sound and spotted Avery Cooper, Jillian's college roommate and the man they'd hired to run Haworth House. With his megawatt smile, he was a sight for sore eyes. She'd had a pretty smileless two weeks.

Tall and broad-shouldered with skin the color of milk chocolate, Avery was his usual impeccably dressed self in a pale gray shirt and black slacks. Gold glinted in the chain around his neck and the hoop on his left ear.

Blinking back a fresh sting of tears, Naomi broke into a run. The moment she reached him, he grabbed her off her feet and swung her around in a huge hug. "This one's from me."

Naomi blinked faster as he set her on her feet and then pulled her close again.

"This one's from your sisters." When he drew back the second time, he studied her more closely. "Love the Jackie O sunglasses and the scarf."

"I used them to sneak out the back door of my apartment." She raised her tote. "I didn't even pack a suitcase. Good thing Jillian insists that we keep some clothes at the hotel. I was so afraid someone would notice and follow me. Not that I don't have a perfect right to leave town. The FBI never told me that I had to stay in Boston. Besides, I just came here to Belle Island. I didn't try to leave the country or anything." She frowned. "I shouldn't feel so guilty about this."

"It's your good-girl syndrome taking over." Avery glanced over her shoulder. "*Did* anyone follow you?"

"I don't think so. For the first time in two weeks, I don't have that prickly feeling at the back of my neck."

"Good." Throwing an arm around her, Avery led her off the dock and along the boardwalk lining the beach area. "Reese and Jillian are bummed that they can't be here."

Truth told, Naomi was a bit relieved about that. After the hubbub of the past two weeks, she was looking forward to some alone time. Jillian was in Europe on a buying trip, and Reese was on a book tour for a cookbook she'd just authored.

"My job is to provide all the TLC they can't shower on you in person. And we're going to start with a late lunch."

"I'm not—"

"Hungry. I know. I know." His tone of voice all sympathy, Avery nevertheless propelled her into a small café on the pier that offered patio seating. "Humor me. Once we get to the hotel, I figure you'll lay low in the tower, and I'll be working."

He pulled a chair out for her at a table that offered a view of the water. At the far end of the island, on a jut of land, she could just see the tower of Haworth House. The tightness inside of her eased.

Avery sat down across from her. "I figure you lost your appetite just about two weeks ago when the BFJ gave you your walking papers."

"BFJ?"

"Big Fat Jerk. When I was getting over Lowell Bidderman, I didn't eat much of anything for nearly a month." He flexed his right arm. "Lost some good muscle tone."

Naomi narrowed her eyes. As far as she knew, Avery had been in a relationship with his current partner, Matt Trudell, since his college days. "Lowell Bidderman?"

"Junior high. I must have been fourteen. Lowell was my first love, and the reason I discovered I was gay at an early age. But I was afraid to say anything, even to Lowell. In junior high I felt I had to at least pass as a heterosexual. Do you remember your first crush?"

She did, and for a second, Naomi felt heat rise in her face again.

"You're blushing," Avery said. "That good, huh?"

She waved a hand. "It was a crush. All fantasy and no substance."

"The best kind." Avery grinned. "Tell me."

She'd never told anyone.

"Confession is good for the soul," Avery urged.

"It's silly. Not even Reese and Jillian know. But when I was fourteen, I had this super crush on a young priest who'd been assigned to our boarding school."

"Really?" Avery's eyes lit up. "Shades of *The Thorn-*

birds. The young innocent girl, the handsome caring priest, forbidden love…all set against the rugged landscape of Australia. Adored the novel. And Richard Chamberlain in the movie—be still my heart."

Naomi nodded, relaxing a bit when she saw that he wasn't shocked. "Exactly. I'd bought the book and smuggled it into the dorm. I read it by flashlight under the covers. I loved it."

"Forbidden treats are always so much more delicious. Tell me more about this priest."

Naomi spread her hands. "Father Bouchard was assigned to the school. He was young, probably in his early twenties. He was so kind, and he was such a good listener. I could talk to him about anything. I fell hopelessly in love. I used to write about him in my diary every day, and then I would dream about him every night."

And a year ago after she'd opened up that parchment in Hattie Haworth's boudoir and the message had been indelibly printed on her mind, she'd unearthed those diaries and reread every one.

"Details. Give me the details. Did you ever actually do it with the priest—in your dreams?"

Heat burned her cheeks again. She'd fantasized about doing a lot of things—not just in her dreams, but in her diaries, too. "What do you think? I'd read *The Thornbirds*."

"Atta girl. Did you ever tell him what you were feeling?"

Her eyes widened in shock. "No. Of course not. It was all fantasy. Pure fantasy."

"Just like me and Lowell. Except for the priest part."

She nodded. Except for the priest part. But the priest

part had definitely been on the piece of parchment she'd pulled out of Hattie's hatbox. *Now you will experience all of those forbidden pleasures….* And that was what had motivated her to reread the diaries she'd written at fourteen. Then she noticed the expression on Avery's face. "What?"

"Just thinking. You know, there's a priest, a Father Dane MacFarland, who's due to check in to Haworth House today."

"Avery, you can't be—"

He raised both hands, palms outward. "I'm not suggesting anything. Just providing information. Besides, he may be eighty and using a walker."

He accepted a menu from the waitress and flashed her a smile. "We'll have your best bottle of champagne and four lobster rolls."

"Champagne?" Naomi echoed.

He turned his smile on her. "Sisters' orders. My mission is to get you from mourning into celebratory mode ASAP. Before anyone finds you here."

"My sisters are being pushy."

Avery's brows shot up. "Turnabout's fair play. You've been taking care of them and pushing them for a long time."

Her lips curved.

Avery patted her hand. "That's better. They're annoyed that they can't talk to you in person. But since we're pretty sure your phone is being tapped, they want you to have as much privacy here as you can get."

"We were careful not to mention Haworth House when we talked. We have this code we've used since we were kids."

"Right." Avery raised both hands and wiggled his fingers. "They're being very cloak-and-daggerish with me, too, using pay phones and only contacting me on my private line at the hotel."

Naomi sighed. "It's not going to take a Sherlock Holmes to trace me here."

Avery shrugged. "Hey, if using codes and pay phones makes your sisters feel like they're helping, I say it's a good thing. And who knows? Might buy you twenty-four to forty-eight hours of privacy."

The waitress arrived and began the uncorking ritual. Once she'd filled the glasses, Avery raised his. "To the new Naomi Brightman."

Naomi blinked. "I'll be perfectly happy to get the old one back."

"I assumed that old Naomi's bridges are pretty much burned."

"And then some. But there's got to be something I can do to fix that. I haven't let myself think about it." She lifted her glass thoughtfully and her gaze shifted beyond his shoulder to Haworth House. Something inside of her stirred. "I have a feeling that I'll figure something out while I'm here."

"Good plan. All I'm saying is that you should keep your options open. You don't necessarily have to return to your life BMD."

"Before Michael Davenport."

He grinned at her. "You're catching on, sugar. When one door slams shut, another one always opens. Hattie Haworth reinvented herself here. You might as well give it a shot, too. So I'll drink to the new Naomi Brightman."

"Cheers," Naomi said, and they both drank champagne.

"ANYTHING ELSE I can get for you, Father MacFarland?"

Dane glanced up from his book, removed his sunglasses and smiled at the pretty redhead who'd been cheerfully refilling his glass of iced tea for the past hour. "No thanks, Tess."

Except for an introduction to Naomi Brightman. That would be nice. She'd been in her room in the tower for over an hour now. He knew that because he'd kept her in his sights ever since she'd left the ferry. Dane had no doubt that the FBI and the police would soon figure out she'd come to her home on Belle Island. But for now MacFarland Investigations, the firm he ran with his brother Ian, appeared to be the only ones on the scene.

Except for Michael Davenport. Gut instinct told Dane that the swindler was probably already here and would make contact with Naomi soon. And so far, she hadn't been lured out onto the balcony by the breathtaking view.

He handed Tess the bill he'd already signed to his room. "I thought I'd stay here and read for a bit more."

"No prob. During the summer months, the courtyard is one of our most popular spots and it's open to Haworth House guests twenty-four-seven."

Dane considered that providential. The hotel itself was a three-story structure built around an inner courtyard lined with porticoes. One side opened into the lobby, and through an archway on the other, guests could access a stairway that descended to the beach. Dane's location at a table beneath one of the porticoes offered him a perfect view of the balcony that opened off Naomi Brightman's room. So far she hadn't made an appearance, but that might be providential, too. He was going to have to tread carefully with her. She'd already managed to throw him off a bit. It hadn't been a part of his plan to talk to her on the ferry.

But there'd been something about the way she'd looked, standing alone at the railing, and he'd felt the tug of sympathy in every fiber of his being.

He lifted his gaze to her balcony. He'd been in her bedroom two days ago on a reconnaissance mission. Once he'd cracked the primitive code she and her sisters used to communicate and learned that she was definitely coming to Haworth House, he'd assigned a man to watch her apartment in Boston, and he'd taken a quick trip to Belle Island to get the lay of the land.

Tess tucked the leather folder containing his bill into her pocket. "We've never had a priest stay here before."

He and Ian had prepared for that question when Dane had chosen to masquerade as a man of the cloth. "My bishop is interested in finding locations for spiritual retreats."

"Oh, Haworth House has a lot of spaces to retreat to. You should talk to our manager, Mr. Cooper."

He smiled at her. "I'll do that, Tess." More importantly, he intended to talk to Naomi Brightman about it. It would be his initial reason for meeting with her.

"I'm going off the clock until tomorrow morning. Will I see you then?" Tess asked.

"You bet." He'd be here until he got his hands on the elusive Michael Davenport. According to his FBI informant, Naomi Brightman had been quite candid with both the police and the FBI. Davenport had told her that he would be in touch. And every instinct that

Dane had told him the swindling con man would keep his word.

Part of Davenport's method of operation was to use women as either partners or patsies in his schemes. During the last con he'd worked in Kansas City he'd stashed his ill-gotten gains with a woman partner until the heat was off. In the end, he'd gotten away with the money. His partner had ended up dead.

Davenport had stashed something with Naomi this time. Dane was sure of it. Because of her squeaky clean record, he figured her for a patsy, not a partner. But that didn't mean she was in any less danger. What he knew for sure was that Davenport hadn't left the Boston area. In the past fourteen days, he'd been spotted three times. There was only one reason for Michael Davenport to take the risk of hanging around. He didn't have access yet to the one hundred million plus he'd embezzled.

Dane had a three-year-old score to settle with Davenport. This time, nothing would stop him from getting his man.

"See you tomorrow, then, Father." With a salute, Tess whirled and hurried back into the hotel. The bubbly and talkative waitress had provided some background information, but thanks to Ian's meticulous research, there was little that Dane didn't already know about Naomi Brightman and Haworth House.

When his cell phone rang, Dane checked the caller ID and then grinned. Speak of the devil. "What's up?"

"Just checking in," Ian said. "How's the priest thing going?"

"So far, so good."

As an investigator, Dane often assumed different personas. During his early years when he'd been in foster homes or on the street, he'd discovered and honed a chameleon-like talent for becoming whatever was needed to get him out of a jam. The decision in this instance for him to pose as a priest had been influenced by Ian's insight into Naomi Brightman's very Catholic background.

Technically, Ian was his half brother. He'd been nine and Ian seven when their mother had died and they'd been split up by social services. They had two other half siblings—a girl and a boy. Somewhere.

"I've got the waitress completely fooled," Dane said.

Ian gave an appreciative laugh.

Thanks to the family that had adopted him, Ian had become an expert on all things Catholic. And he maintained that Catholic women had an instant trust in priests. They confided in them. Ian swore his adoptive mother had been "best buds" with a whole string of parish priests. Dane's only experience with women and their relationships with priests was the second season of *The Sopranos,* when Tony's wife had been really chummy with one.

"I have yet to put this little masquerade to the test. I haven't seen her since I arrived, and I still have to wangle an introduction."

"It's going to work like a charm. You'll see."

Dane was banking on it. He'd gone along with Ian because he needed a cover that would allow him to win Naomi Brightman's trust in a short amount of time. The sooner he figured out just how she fit into Davenport's scheme, the better. And he needed to be close by when Davenport contacted her.

Plus, posing as a priest might also help him with his other problem. He'd felt a connection to Naomi Bright-man even before he'd seen her in person. That wasn't like him at all. Long ago, he'd learned to keep an emotional distance between himself and any case he was working.

He'd decided that the reason for his reaction to her was because they'd both experienced the responsibility of being the oldest sibling. Of course, their stories were vastly different. She'd never been separated from her sisters, and he'd lost everyone.

He shifted his eyes to the balcony outside her bedroom. But when he'd first seen her in the flesh, his reaction had gone far beyond empathy. A raw sexual awareness had shot through him like a lance. It was a purely visceral response that he couldn't seem to control. And the experience had repeated itself in one way or another each time he'd seen her since.

At first he'd tried to prevent it, then he'd tried to analyze it. Finally he'd settled for trying to get used to it.

And that wasn't going very smoothly. He'd very nearly reached out to touch her when he'd talked to her on the ferry. The urge to lay a hand on her arm or on the side of her face had been so strong. As a priest, he'd have to keep that impulse in check.

"You still there, Dane?"

"Yeah." Annoyed with himself, he dragged his eyes away from Naomi's balcony.

"For a moment there, I thought I'd lost you. I take it you haven't seen our other friend, either?"

"You'll be the first to know. He wasn't on the ferry." But Dane hadn't expected him to be. The man was smart. He'd have known that Naomi would come to Haworth House just as Dane had known. In the year since she and her sisters had purchased the hotel, this was the only place Naomi Brightman had escaped to.

It was a matter of time before Davenport showed. The island held a myriad of places for a secret rendezvous.

There was a brief pause, then Ian said, "Things are slow here at the office. I'm bored."

Dane could picture his brother. He'd be sitting at his desk, feet propped up, wearing cutoff shorts and a T-shirt and shooting wadded-up balls of paper at the wastebasket strategically placed five feet away. When Dane had located Ian a year ago, he'd been seated behind a desk at the CIA wearing a suit, tie and a very serious expression on his face. It was the same face that Dane remembered from his childhood. But in the short time they'd worked together, the formerly uptight Ian had loosened up quite a bit.

"You know field work has its boring days. Don't forget I'm just off two weeks of shadowing." There hadn't been much excitement in keeping Naomi Brightman under surveillance. In spite of the fact that her life had been thrown into major turmoil, she'd stuck as much as she could to a daily routine. She'd bought her latte at the same coffee shop each day. She'd arrived at her office and left at the same time. Except on Tuesdays. That was the day she worked late. Even her wardrobe had a routine to it. Though the colors might vary, she always wore a suit, and in addition to a briefcase, she carried the same enormous tote bag everywhere. She'd even had it with her when he'd talked to her on the ferry.

"Ian." At the memory, Dane straightened in his chair. "There is something that you can look into for me."

"I'm all ears."

"I spoke briefly with Naomi on the ferry just as we were about to disembark. We didn't exchange names or anything. Just a few casual words between strangers. But she thought she knew me. It shook her up. She asked if I'd been a priest at that boarding school she went to in France. Do you think you can dig up something on that?"

"Is the Pope Catholic? I'll be in touch. And if things start to heat up on the island, let me know. I'll gladly provide backup."

"Will do." After repocketing his cell phone, Dane stretched out his legs and crossed them at the ankles. There was no one better at digging up information than Ian. With his brother's help, Dane had no doubt that they would locate their younger sibs very soon. The little ones had been four and two on the day their mother had died and their life as a family had ended.

Dane put his sunglasses on and gazed out at the sea. Sharon MacFarland had been twenty-eight when her life had been snuffed out, a year younger than he was now. He remembered her as a good mother. She'd loved them. The problem was she'd had a dream that one day she'd find her Prince Charming. And Lord knows, she'd looked for him. Persistence had been Sharon MacFarland's middle name. He and his three other siblings all had different fathers, and none of them had turned out to be the prince his mother was looking for.

A tingle of awareness moved through him. And Dane knew before he raised his eyes to the balcony that Naomi would be there. The moment that he looked at her, the awareness sharpened and he felt an irresistible pull.

Before he was even conscious of the decision, he rose from his chair and moved closer to the edge of the open courtyard to get a clearer view.

She stood at a waist-high railing, looking out at the sea. Though he couldn't see them, he knew what her legs looked like, and he recalled the strength and athleticism in the way she moved. If he closed his eyes, he could recall every detail of the features that had been captured in her photo on King and Fairchild Web site. Gray-green eyes, pale skin with just a sprinkling of freckles, a straight, narrow nose, strong cheekbones and a chin that hinted at stubbornness.

But there was something different about her today. She had the same serious look on her face that she'd worn for the past two weeks. But he sensed less tension. Her shoulders were more relaxed and her hands rested on the balcony rather than gripping it.

That was when it struck him. Her hair—that was different, too. It fell loose to her shoulders, and the late-afternoon sun haloed it around her head. That had to be why he'd never noted the fiery red highlights before. His eyes narrowed then, focusing on her face. Her lips were moving. Not even a hint of a sound drifted to him. Was she whispering? Praying?

For a moment a vivid image flashed into his mind. She was in his arms, her cheek pressed against his, her breath hot in his ear. She was whispering to him. His blood heated, his pulse raced. He couldn't make out her words above the pounding of his heart. Then her eyes shifted suddenly to him, and her gaze moved slowly up his body. He hadn't thought it possible for his body to grow any harder, but it did.

When her eyes finally locked on his, there was a moment—an instant, he would convince himself later—when he couldn't think of anything, anyone but her. And he barely blocked the urge to walk into the courtyard and climb up the stone wall to her balcony.

The thought was so ridiculous that it cleared his mind immediately. Who did he think he was? A comic book hero? Or Shakespeare's hormone-driven Romeo?

Still, he wasn't the one who broke the spell by walking away. It was Naomi Brightman who turned from the railing and disappeared into her room.

2

THE MOMENT NAOMI entered the suite she and her sisters shared, she felt a bit more of her tension ease. Lunch and champagne with Avery had been fun, but this was really where she wanted to be.

Slipping out of her shoes and dropping her tote bag on the bed, she moved to the love seats facing each other in front of a bay window. A gift basket sat on the small coffee table. Opening it, she found a box of candy, a business card from the village of Belle Bay and two notes.

The first one was from Reese.

Naomi,
Sorry we can't be there. Jillian and I have asked Avery to take very good care of you. The one thing we're sure of is that you're going to get past this. All of our lives, we've seen you set goals for yourself and meet them. We can't wait to see what you'll do next. The chocolate is to inspire you to indulge yourself.
And don't forget what you always told me when

I was small and didn't think I would ever reach my goal. "Little steps. Just take little steps."
Love,
Reese

Naomi blinked, the back of her eyes burning. She knew without opening the small box that it would contain the special chocolate truffles Reese had created as a trademark confection for Haworth House. Chocolates were Naomi's weakness, so she rationed her consumption. In a stressful job, it paid off to eat healthy. Her youngest sister had always considered chocolate good therapy. Then she reread the note. *We can't wait to see what you'll do next.*

But what if the thing she wanted most was to go back to her old job and her old life—before Michael Davenport? Little steps were good advice if she just knew where she was headed….

With a sigh, she picked up the next note.

Naomi,
Avery is always telling me "When a door closes, another door opens." I hope that by coming to Haworth House you'll figure out how to open that door. The place has opened up a whole new career for me.

The business card is from a new boutique in the village called Discoveries. I was thinking that you might want a different wardrobe for when you decide to open that door. And, hey, shopping is the best way I know to destress and get your mind ready to explore new paths.
Love,
Jillian

Blinking again, Naomi studied the card. Discoveries, owned and operated by Molly Pepperman, promised the latest in fashions.

Obviously, her sisters and Avery were on the same page in pushing her toward a fresh start. And she agreed with them in part. She wanted to discover who the new Naomi Brightman was going to be herself.

But so far she didn't have a clue. And how could she be positive that she wanted to leave the old Naomi Brightman behind? After all, they'd traveled a long road together. How was she supposed to change from the person she'd been all her life into someone…she didn't even know?

Little steps.

Her gaze fell on the huge tote bag she carried with her everywhere. If she wanted a new beginning, she could start by getting rid of her tote. She'd had it since she'd started college nine years ago, and it held everything that was absolutely essential to her life. Most people used a filing cabinet, but she carted that tote around like some sort of a security blanket. Or obsession.

Periodically—say, once a year—she'd sort through it, but almost always when she discarded something, she stuffed in something else she wanted to keep at her fingertips.

And it weighed a ton. Hefting it up, she turned it over and dumped the contents out on the bed. Then she simply stared. There was a day planner and three notebooks—she never went into meetings or court without one. Then there was her makeup bag, an extra pair of earrings, a change purse, a wallet and all of the little surprise gifts Michael had given her in the six months they'd known each other.

Somewhere in the roller coaster of emotions she'd

experienced in the two weeks since she'd walked into
Leo King's office and been introduced to the two FBI
agents, she'd tried to figure out if what she'd felt for
Michael Davenport had been love.

Or had she simply been dazzled by the attention he'd
paid her?

No one had ever treated her the way Michael had, as
if she were special. She picked up the souvenir key chain
he'd given her on their last night together. It boasted
two charms, a silver key to Boston and a crystal heart.
When he'd presented it to her, he'd asked for her keys
and he'd transferred them to the new chain so that she
would always carry the key to his heart.

The gesture and the words were so typically Michael.
He was the perfect gentleman. He'd taken charge of their
relationship from that first chance meeting in the Four
Seasons and he'd made all the decisions.

That had been part of his attraction, she supposed.
As the oldest, she'd often played a decision-making role
when it came to her sisters. And Michael had lifted that
burden off her shoulders. He'd even taken charge of the
physical side of their relationship. He'd told her that
considering her background, he wanted to take things
slowly with her.

Very slowly, to her way of thinking. They'd shared
long kisses, even some heavy petting in his private limo.
But in the six months she'd known him, they'd never
actually made love. She'd thought of objecting more
than once, but she hadn't. It was so much easier to be
just swept along.

Would she have been more aggressive if she'd felt
differently about him, she wondered now, or maybe if
there'd been more heat between them?

She'd given her engagement ring to the authorities to

help pay back some of the people Michael had swindled. But she'd held on to the trinkets. Originally, he'd asked her to keep them so that when they were old and gray, they could take them out and rekindle memories of their early days together.

At the time the idea had moved her and she'd promised to keep all of them. Forever. Was that why she'd taken them from her apartment and brought them to Belle Island? Or was she still nursing some adolescent hope that the stories about Michael would turn out to be false, that he would get in touch with her again as he'd promised?

Whirling, she strode away from the bed and then paced back to it. What in the world was wrong with her? The memories were all lies. Why couldn't she accept that? She stared down at the little mementos. She should toss them. But for tonight she wasn't going to put too much pressure on herself. *Little steps.*

After rescuing her makeup, cell phone and wallet, she scooped the rest of the items on the bed back into the tote. She wasn't quite ready to throw it out, but if she kept it in the suite, she might be tempted to use it again.

To prevent that, she strode to Jillian's closet. Having a sister who was a shopaholic—and a generous one—came in handy at times. Naomi chose a small handbag from the collection, one that would hold her hotel key card, wallet and cell phone. She knew that Jillian wouldn't mind lending her the bag, especially since it was for a good cause. The new Naomi Brightman was no longer going to drag around a tote.

She suddenly thought of a place she could store it temporarily. Grabbing the tote and her keys, she left her room and strode down the hall to the carved oak door that led to Hattie's old bedroom. After opening it, she climbed the circular iron staircase to the second level.

During the rehab, they'd built a partition to divide the room into two spaces; one side was furnished as a sitting area with sofas and chairs, and the other as an office with three desks. They all shared Reese's computer.

Locating the lever on the inner wall, she pulled it and watched the door to Hattie's secret room spring open. Without even turning on the light, she set the tote inside. Then she hesitated, catching sight of the fantasy box on the floor. For a moment she was tempted, just as she was each time she returned to Haworth House, to choose another parchment. If she picked a different fantasy, could she stop obsessing about the priest one?

No. She pulled the lever and watched the door close. She wasn't going to think about it. Not today. *Little steps,* she reminded herself as she hurried back to her bedroom. Tonight she was going to let Haworth House work its magic on her. Moving out to her balcony, she rested her hands on the railing and gazed out to the sea. This was a ritual with her each time she came here. The sight of the water calmed her and helped her to refocus. The sun felt warm on her face, and after a few moments, she recalled a prayer from her childhood. "Please," she breathed, "let me find a way to do what has to be done."

She'd learned the prayer from Father Pierre Bouchard. He'd shared it with her during one of their conversations in the sacristy, and it had quickly become her private mantra. Usually, the focus of her prayers had to do with her sisters. Today, the prayer was for herself.

"Let me find a way to discover the new Naomi Brightman."

There. She'd said it. And as she stood in the late-afternoon sunshine, she repeated it again and again.

The first awareness that she was being watched had her stomach plummeting. She dropped her gaze to the courtyard below her. A few of the tables had filled and a waitress was balancing drinks on a tray as she crossed the flagstones.

No one seemed to be looking in her direction. Had she been mistaken? The hairs on the back of her neck didn't think so, and they'd been working overtime lately.

The slant of the afternoon sun left one of the porticoes in shadow. That was why she saw his legs first. Considering the time it took her gaze to travel up them, she reached two conclusions. They were long and he was tall. Very tall. The black T-shirt did nothing to hide the flat chest, well-muscled arms and broad shoulders.

Suddenly curious, she shifted her attention to his face. Though it was partially in shadow, she caught an impression of leanness, a sharp slash of cheekbones and a dark shadow along his jaw that gave him a rugged look. Recognition rippled through her.

It was the stranger who'd spoken to her on the boat. The one who'd made her think of Father Bouchard.

Without the hooded sweatshirt, she could see that his hair was jet-black and mussed by the wind. And his eyes. He wasn't wearing the sunglasses, but at this distance, all she could tell was that they appeared dark and were definitely aimed at her. Awareness skittered along her nerve endings, and for a moment, she couldn't seem to drag her gaze away from him.

What was wrong with her? He was a stranger. And he was looking at her as intently as she was looking at him. *Devouring* was the word that came to mind. She was sure she'd never even thought of devouring a man with her eyes before. But wasn't that exactly what she was doing now? And there was a part of her that wanted to do more than think about it. Her pulse raced, and she felt a little breathless, as if she'd just run up the long flight of stairs from the beach.

It was then that he stepped fully into the courtyard, and she saw what she hadn't seen before.

A Roman collar.

For a moment, her heart stopped. Her knees went weak, and heat flooded her body. The man she'd just been devouring with her eyes was a priest. He didn't just look like the priest she'd fantasized about when she was fourteen. He *was* a priest. And the realization had shot the attraction she'd been experiencing into overdrive.

No. This was not going to happen to her again. Willing her legs to work, she turned away from the railing and made it to one of the small love seats before she collapsed.

Leaning back against the cushions, she stared straight ahead, forcing herself to concentrate on the details—the pale green paint she'd selected under Jillian's direction, the oriental rug with its pastel colors, the gleam of the honey-colored wood beneath. Gradually, the image of the man—the priest—she'd just seen in the courtyard dimmed, and a flame of anger burst to life inside of her.

This was all due to that piece of parchment paper she'd drawn out of Hattie's box. Her fantasy crush on Father Bouchard had happened so long ago, and she'd outgrown it. She'd been a young, impressionable fourteen when she'd read *The Thornbirds*. That was when the idea of making love with a priest had first taken hold of her.

All the girls at the school had had a crush on Father Bouchard. The confessional had never been busier. One would have thought from the long lines that Our Lady of Solace boarding school had become a den of iniquity. She'd even figured out how to spend extra time with the young priest by volunteering to clean the sacristy each day after he'd said Mass. That was when he always lingered and found the time to listen to her. And talk to her. Later she would record in her diary each word he said, no matter how casual, and each smile he gave to her.

In her mind, in that place where fantasy/puppy love flourished, she'd fallen in love with Father Pierre Bouchard. She'd even taken to writing her name as *Naomi Bouchard* over and over again in her diary and notebooks. All simple, innocent things.

In the beginning, the fantasies she'd spun in her mind about Father Bouchard had also been innocent—taking long walks, their hands and arms brushing occasionally. But the heat that had rushed through her at every imaginary contact hadn't been so innocent.

And eventually, her fantasies had become more explicit, at least as explicit as she'd been able to spin them at fourteen. And even though she knew it had to be a sin to continue to indulge in them, she'd never confessed them to anyone. Until today when she'd told Avery.

When Father Bouchard was transferred to a small parish near Monte Carlo, she'd cried herself to sleep for weeks. But the fantasies had gradually faded. She'd put them out of her mind years ago. Up until the day she'd drawn that parchment paper out of Hattie Haworth's hatbox.

THE MOMENT NAOMI disappeared into her room, Dane cursed himself silently. Ms. Brightman was definitely going to be a problem for him.

Bottom line—he wanted her. And she was his best link to the man he was determined to find. Anyone who thought you could mix business with pleasure didn't make a successful businessman.

With an inward sigh, he faced what he'd known from the first moment he'd set eyes on her. This was not going to be a simple job. At the top of the list of possible complications was the fact that he was impersonating a priest. His game plan was to convince Naomi to confide in him. That would call for some up-close-and-personal time with the woman.

And even if he was tempted, as he already was, to make a pass at her, to do so could blow his cover and cost him what chance he had of nabbing Michael Davenport.

She's off-limits, MacFarland. He'd just have to get more deeply into the role of being a priest. Think holy and celibate thoughts. His ability to assume different personas had always been his primary survival skill. And to be forewarned was to be forearmed.

The laughter pierced his concentration first. But it was only when a young couple entered the courtyard from the steps to the beach that Dane realized he hadn't moved since Naomi Brightman had disappeared from the balcony. And he hadn't taken his gaze from the open door to her room.

Was he waiting, hoping for her to come back out?

Way to go, MacFarland. Disgusted, he strode to the entrance of the main lobby. He had a job to do. And step one was to arrange a personal meeting with Naomi Brightman. He spotted Avery Cooper behind the registration desk and started toward him. Avery might look more like a bouncer in an upscale club, but according to the research Ian had done, the man had graduated top of his class from Harvard Business School. And from what Dane had gathered from their reunion at the pier, he was a friend to Naomi. That made Avery Cooper a good man to have on his side.

And the perfect man to arrange his first meeting with Naomi. Tomorrow, Dane decided. That would give her time to settle in, and it would buy him a little time to get deeper into his role.

As a priest, Dane reminded himself. A very celibate priest.

3

"YOU'RE SURE you don't mind?" Avery had arrived with her room service order and they'd shared a meal and some wine. Now he lounged on one of the love seats, his long legs extended beyond the edge of the coffee table that separated them. "It's not too late to change your mind."

"I'm sure I want to meet with Father MacFarland in the morning." And she was. However, Naomi noted that Avery didn't look completely convinced. That was entirely due to her initial reaction to his news that Father Dane MacFarland had requested a personal meeting with her in the morning.

She'd dropped the wineglass she'd been holding, then she'd cut one of her fingers in her hurried attempt to pick up the shattered shards.

And that had made her angry enough that she'd immediately agreed to meet with the priest. In fact, she'd insisted on it. She was not going to allow herself to get caught up again in a ridiculous adolescent fantasy. After all, she was an adult woman. An attorney. She'd been engaged to a man she'd thought she loved.

And then she'd been dumped and fired. Was it any wonder her nerves were on edge? A lesser woman might have had some kind of breakdown. Or at least asked her personal physician for some really good drugs.

Instead, she'd come to Haworth House to put her life back together. And she wasn't going to hide out in her room simply because of…a priest.

"Father MacFarland seems to be a charming man," Avery said. "If Tess hadn't spilled the beans that one of the owners was in residence this week, I might have been able to handle it myself. But he specifically requested you. And his idea of booking a block of rooms together with conference space to hold spiritual retreats as a recruiting device for new seminarians is brilliant."

"Doesn't the church already have facilities for holding retreats?" Naomi asked.

"Sure." Avery spread his hands. "But there's a growing shortage of priests in the United States, and Father MacFarland is hoping a venue like this will increase attendance."

"And you began to hear the little echoes of *cha-ching, cha-ching* in the back of your mind."

Avery grinned at her. "Well, that, too. If Father Mac-Farland likes the place, it could be very profitable for the hotel in the off-season."

"I'm happy to talk with him," Naomi said. "In fact, it could be good for me. I haven't been out of the tower floors since I got here."

"Then I'm happy I let myself get carried away," Avery said as he rose. He glanced at his watch. "I'll ring the good father's room and let him know that it's all arranged—ten o'clock tomorrow morning in the courtyard. One more thing." He reached into his pocket and pulled out a set of keys.

Naomi glanced at them. "What?"

"If we're going to get you out of your room, you'll need transportation. As long as you're on the island, I want you to have full access to my car."

Her eyes widened. "Your Corvette?"

"That would be the one."

Naomi knew how much he treasured his car. "Avery, I can use the car Jillian keeps here if I want to go into town."

He moved toward her, took her hand and dropped the keys into her palm. "Think of driving it as part of your exploration of discovering the new Naomi Brightman. I've always found when something's troubling me, a fast ride in a car with the top down helps, and it's a lot cheaper than therapy. Try it."

"Okay." She threw her arms around Avery and hugged him. "Thanks."

Stepping back, he grinned down at her. "Enjoy. And since my mission here is accomplished for tonight, I'll get my nose back to the grindstone."

The moment Avery left, Naomi locked the door and turned around. While they'd eaten, the sky had darkened, and the only illumination in the room came from the moonlight streaming through the filmy curtain she'd drawn across the closed balcony doors.

Another surge of anger at herself had her pacing to the balcony doors and throwing them open. It was bad enough that she'd run away from her troubles in Boston. She was not going to allow herself to hide out in her room. That was not the way she was going to explore who the new Naomi Brightman was.

That's when she saw him. He was in a room directly across from hers and one level down. Naomi's throat went dry. The doors to his balcony were open, and the drapes billowed inward. Because he had the lights on, the thin material of the curtains had become transparent, and she could see him very clearly.

There was no Roman collar now, nothing to indicate he was a priest. But she recognized that body. And this time she could see a whole lot more of it. He wore only a towel around his waist as he strode across the room and picked up a phone.

He stood with his back to her, his dark hair wet and slicked back, his broad shoulders still glistening from a shower.

Her mouth literally watered as her eyes traveled down the well-muscled back to his waist. The towel was short and damp and clung like a second skin to the curves of his tight butt. It would be hard to the touch, she thought, then marveled at the tingling rush of heat in her fingers. She wanted to touch him. She wanted to run her hands over every plane and hard angle of that body.

And she wanted to taste him, too.

As she thought of doing both of those things, her insides melted. She couldn't feel her legs below her knees, but she discovered that all on their own, they'd moved her to the railing of her balcony.

She continued to stare, fascinated by the angle of his arm, the strength in his wrist, the grace of his movement as he lowered the phone to its stand. And then she saw it. Lying right next to the phone. The Roman collar. And that should have had the effect of stepping into a cold shower.

But it didn't. Instead, everything she was feeling intensified. Her pulse hammered at her wrists, at the base of her throat. The heat she'd felt from the moment she'd spotted him ratcheted up several degrees. Her brain cells clicked off, and she forgot to breathe.

When he turned and met her eyes, she suddenly couldn't think. All she knew was desire—a scorching wave of it that she couldn't control. Didn't want to. What she was feeling wasn't anything like the illicit puppy love she'd experienced at fourteen.

She wasn't sure how long she stood there or how long she might have remained on her balcony, but the fact that someone had knocked on her door finally penetrated. It had to be room service come to clear the dishes, she thought as she turned and moved on legs she still couldn't feel.

But when she opened the door, there was no one in sight. Just an envelope lying on the floor. She blinked, still trying to clear her head as she leaned over to pick it up. She'd closed and locked the door and made it back to her bed before it sank in.

The envelope was made of the same yellowing parchment that she'd pulled out of Hattie's box in the secret room.

And she knew even before she opened the envelope what the folded piece of parchment inside would say.

Your secret fantasy has always been to make love with a priest. Now you will experience all those forbidden pleasures.

NAOMI GLANCED at her watch, then pressed a hand against the nerves dancing in her stomach. Nine forty-six. Exactly two minutes since the last time she'd checked. Too early to go down to the courtyard. With a quick, impatient step, she strode to her closet and inspected her image in the mirror.

For the fifth time.

It hadn't improved. She still looked like a lawyer. The linen suit was a pearl-gray color and the white silk tank top she wore beneath it was prim and suitable for the office. Normally, she liked neutral colors. In fact, her entire wardrobe was a tribute to the practicality of the word *neutral*.

So why was *drab* the word that came to mind now? It was the perfect suit to wear to court in Boston in the summer. And dammit, she was a lawyer. Not to mention a hotel owner.

Lifting her chin, she stared at herself defiantly. She was appropriately dressed for a business meeting. None of the more casual outfits she kept here at Haworth House—T-shirts, a couple pairs of shorts, a bathing suit and some jeans—would do for a meeting with a prospective client. And certainly not a priest.

Pressing her hands to her temples, Naomi walked back to the side of her bed and sank down on it. Never in her life had she taken such care, never had she worried so much about how she looked. Not for the office. Not for a court appearance. Not for Michael Davenport.

Not even for herself.

Perhaps that was the problem. Maybe to become the new Naomi, she had to focus more on pleasing herself. Pulling open the top drawer of the bedside table, she glanced at the parchment envelope she'd placed there the night before. She had no idea how it had ended up on the floor outside of her bedroom.

Had Hattie put it there? That had been her first suspicion. But the only manifestation she had experienced of her presence was on that day in Hattie's boudoir when she and her sisters had toasted their purchase of Haworth House with champagne.

There'd been nothing since. Not even a little chill in the air. Still, Naomi had often felt her presence.

A less fanciful explanation would be that Jillian had confided in Avery about the hatbox and the secret room. And since he now knew just who her first crush had been, he might have somehow dug out the parchment and left it for her. As a joke? Or as another little incentive to live on the wild side, like giving her the keys to his Corvette. Avery might think that doing something as outrageous as seducing a priest could be just the ticket to jettison her down the road to reinventing herself.

Whoever was responsible, receiving the parchment with her fantasy written on it had helped her to think everything through and reach a decision. Since she'd locked the tote with her notebooks in Hattie's secret room, she'd used the hotel stationery to jot her ideas down.

Making love with a priest was a particularly alluring fantasy because it was so forbidden. And impossible. Talk about being star-crossed. Absolute secrecy was another essential element of the fantasy. When she was fourteen, the fact that no one knew about her crush on Father Bouchard had been ninety percent of the thrill.

Most of the guilty pleasure she'd experienced had been private, the result of writing those diary entries by flashlight in the middle of the night and those vivid and tantalizing dreams she'd had after she'd fallen asleep. During the day, she'd been very careful to act in a perfectly respectful and normal way around the young priest.

And there was absolutely no reason why she couldn't handle the attraction she was feeling for Father Dane MacFarland the same way. If the intensity of the attraction persisted, she would record everything she imagined she might do to him in her diary, and make sure the fantasy stayed right there on the page.

Before she'd fallen asleep, she'd considered going up to Hattie's secret room and retrieving one of her notebooks out of her tote bag. But they were a part of her old life. Right after her meeting with Father Mac-Farland this morning, she'd go into town and buy some new notebooks to record her new fantasies.

And she already had one to record—the dream she'd had during the night. Even now as the memory slipped into her mind, Naomi felt her eyes close and her breathing become more rapid.

It had been dark in her bedroom. The moon had shifted in the sky, so only starlight had filtered through the curtains. But she'd known that the figure standing just inside her balcony doors was him. She'd known it by the sensory shock her body experienced.

He'd stood there, his dark hair slicked back, wearing nothing but the skimpy towel she'd seen him in the night before. The towel that she'd wanted very much to rip off him.

The urge to get out of bed and cross to him was strong. But the dream seemed to paralyze her, and all she'd been able to do was push herself into a sitting position. She couldn't even lift her hands, and her voice hadn't worked. All she could do was look at him as a rush of hunger seared through her. The needy ache that followed freed one of her hands and she lifted it to beckon him closer.

He moved then from the faint illumination of starlight into the deeper shadows of the room. Flames licked along her nerve endings and a hotter fire burst to life inside her. He knelt on the bed, took the hand she still held extended and drew her to her knees. They knelt facing each other, their bodies nearly brushing. That was when she saw it—the thin strip of white at his throat. It made such a stark contrast to the bronze tone of his skin. Raising her free hand, she ran her fingers over the stiff material of the Roman collar and felt the shocking thrill move through her.

This was wrong. So wrong. Was that why she wanted it so desperately? Raising her eyes, she met his. They were so hot that when he dropped his gaze to her mouth, she felt her lips burn.

Finding the strength to move, she dug her fingers into his shoulder to draw him closer. He settled his at her waist. Together they moved until their bodies touched. Pleasure exploded at each contact point. Her breasts and thighs ached where they softened against his muscles.

He rocked into her and she felt the length of his erection sink into the skin of her stomach. *Wrong. So wrong,* she thought as heat rocketed through her with the speed of a wildfire.

More. She remembered then what she'd thought of doing earlier and she ran her hands to the back of his waist to slip her fingers beneath that towel. His muscles were tighter than she'd imagined. She kneaded them first, then dug her nails into them.

In response, the exact one she'd wanted, his hands gripped her waist and lifted her. She wrapped her legs around him and wiggled until his erection was pressed flush against the raging heat at her center. There were still barriers separating them—the towel and the prim cotton of her bikini panties. But she couldn't bear for him to stop moving, couldn't make herself stop. Instead, she gave herself over to the building wave of pleasure until she finally crested and let herself be tossed over.

When she'd awakened, he was gone. Because all he'd been was a fantasy.

Ignoring the piercing sense of loss, Naomi opened her eyes. Even the memory of the intense pleasure she'd experienced in her dream had weakened her so that she had to brace herself with her hands or she would have collapsed on the bed.

It was sad but true. The fantasy sex she'd had with her imaginary Father MacFarland had beat out any sex she'd ever had with a real man. The new Naomi was going to have to do something about that.

She let her gaze stray to the foot of the bed where her T-shirt and panties lay folded. The one regret she had was that she hadn't worn more accessible clothing in her dream. She was going to remedy that, too. It wasn't only notebooks that she intended to purchase in town today. She was going to visit the boutique Jillian had recommended.

Shifting her gaze to the parchment envelope, Naomi pushed the drawer shut and drew in a deep breath. She'd made the right decision. She was going to continue to indulge her fantasy. Hadn't she gotten the best night's sleep she'd had in weeks?

Handling challenging situations and keeping in control had always been two of her strengths. All she had to do was keep her daytime meetings with Father MacFarland brief and businesslike. Then in the dark hours of the night, she was going to indulge herself with no-holds-barred, wild sex. As hot as she could possibly imagine it. And she was going to record every single detail in her diary.

It was a simple plan. And who could it harm?

Rising, she glanced at her watch. Nine fifty-five. She scooped up the small purse she'd borrowed from

Jillian's room and the keys to Avery's car. Time to go meet Father MacFarland.

WHEN HIS CELL RANG, Michael Davenport shifted the hedge clipper to his right hand and managed to answer it on the second ring. The voice at the other end was impatient.

"Do you have it yet?"

"No, I haven't even made contact yet." Michael kept the annoyance out of his voice.

"Why not?"

Michael bit back a sigh. He preferred to work alone. However, in this case, since he'd been recognized, he'd been faced with the choice of either working with a partner or abandoning a very lucrative project. He'd chosen the former. And he was going to maintain the illusion of the partnership until he could foresee a way out. "Patience, my friend."

There was annoyed grumbling on the other end of the line.

To Michael's way of thinking, the partner element only added spice to his endgame—relieving Naomi Brightman of the hundred million he'd temporarily stashed with her. "Every time you contact me, you increase the chances of someone locating me. Then you'll be plumb out of luck since I'm the only one who knows where the money is."

More grumbling.

Tucking the phone under his ear, he repositioned the clippers and continued to trim the hedge that bordered the maze on the garden side of the hotel. There wasn't much chance that the throwaway cell phone would be traced, but he was working with an amateur.

"When will you have it?"

"Soon. She got to Belle Island yesterday afternoon," he said as he rounded off the end of the hedge. "I was in town when she disembarked." He could have added that from his position right now he could see the bay window in her room. But the less his partner knew, the better. "She was picked up and transported to her hotel by the manager, Avery Cooper. I can't contact her while she's in the hotel. There's too great a risk she's being watched or that someone might recognize me."

At least that was what he wanted his partner to believe. But now that Naomi was on the island, he just had to bide his time for the right moment.

"You're going to have to let me play this my way," he added.

"Your way or the highway," the voice said tightly.

Exactly. But Michael managed to keep the smile out of his voice when he said, "Look, we both want the same thing here."

"And we'd have it if you hadn't been so greedy. We should have ended this weeks ago."

Michael refrained from pointing out that his greed had netted them huge profits.

"You should never have given it to her," the voice accused. "We could have the money in an offshore account by now."

"And the Feds would know just where it is. And there are people who are much better at tracking large sums of money than the U.S. government. Once they located it, they'd know how to trace it if either of us tried to withdraw it. I know what I'm doing."

And he did. She'd brought the money to the island. Her predictability had all but guaranteed it. All he had to do was bide his time until he could safely make his move. Patience was a quality that paid off in his line of work. The perfect opportunity would present itself.

"I'll give you two days. If you don't have it by then, I'm going to the police and I'll tell them where you are."

Michael sighed as he disconnected the call. It was an empty threat, he knew. But it was a sign that his idiot partner was near panic. That was why partners never seemed to work out for him. He'd have to dispose of this one just as he had his last one.

But not yet. Two days gave him plenty of time to make contact with Naomi and he wasn't about to be rushed. This was the part of his work that he loved the most.

4

"HERE ARE YOUR LATTES." Tess set them in front of Dane with a flourish. "And I'll bring the scones just as soon as Ms. Brightman arrives. Can I get you anything else, Father MacFarland?"

"Not at the moment."

As Tess hurried away, Dane leaned back in his chair and glanced at his watch. Nine fifty-eight. If he'd learned anything at all about Naomi Brightman in the past two weeks, it was that she was punctual. And as the time approached, the nerves in his stomach tightened.

Dane knew how to handle women. He'd been doing it for a long time. And he'd handle this one. How many times had he assured himself of that during the long sleepless night he'd spent? And how many times had he wiped damp palms against the sheets because he'd been fantasizing about just how he might handle her.

Dammit, he wanted to touch her. There'd been that moment last evening when he'd stepped out of his shower and turned to see her watching him. The surge of desire had been unprecedented, nearly uncontrollable. He'd wanted to go to her. And the fact that she was only minutes away at the other side of the hotel, the certain knowledge that he could be inside her room, inside her within minutes, had nearly blurred his judgment long enough for him to make a mistake.

Dane MacFarland didn't like to make mistakes. And he was going to make damn sure the attractive Ms. Brightman didn't lure him into making one today. He just had to remember who he was. Role-playing was his strength.

As she stepped into the courtyard, Dane felt that intense sensory awareness ripple through him again. And as she drew closer, desire tightened hot and hard in him. Not good. *Get a grip, MacFarland. You can't afford to spook her.*

Clearing his mind, he used the technique he'd relied on ever since that fateful day when he'd been separated from his brothers and sister. He put all thoughts of Dane MacFarland out of his mind and became the role he was playing. But even a priest might not be able to prevent himself from enjoying the grace of her walk, the way those slim, strong legs ate up the ground. She was wearing one of her trim, dull-colored business suits and sensible shoes, and she'd pulled her hair back into a bun.

As Father MacFarland, he allowed himself to enjoy the way the wind teased some strands loose, but Dane couldn't quite prevent himself from thinking how enjoyable it might be to tease the rest free until the sun could halo the red-gold mass around her head again.

Rising from his chair as she reached the table, he refocused all his energy on the role he was playing. He was Father MacFarland.

More than once on the walk across the courtyard, Naomi had been tempted to just turn and run. She'd already experienced what this priest could do to her with a look, and how her newly discovered overactive imagination could build on that. But she was going to focus on keeping the meeting brief. Surely it wouldn't take long to answer his questions and show him the conference space. She'd let Avery negotiate the money part of it.

Then she'd drive the Corvette into town, buy some new clothes and a stack of notebooks and prepare to indulge her fantasy.

"Ms. Brightman, I didn't realize who you were when we spoke on the ferry, nor that we'd be meeting again so soon. I'm Father MacFarland." He took off the sunglasses he was wearing. The blue-gray eyes they'd covered were kind and a bit curious. There was no trace of the heat that she'd experienced in her fantasy or that she'd felt across the length of the courtyard yesterday. It was almost as if the man she was looking at now was an entirely different person. The knot that had formed in her stomach the moment she'd left her room tightened.

"I'm happy to meet you, Father," she said as she gripped his hand. "I understand you're interested in the facilities Haworth House has to offer."

"Yes, I am. This is quite a beautiful spot you've got here."

His smile held the same warmth as his eyes, but the heat of his palm as it pressed against hers sent heat arrowing right down to her toes. Memories of her dream flooded her system, drying her throat and clouding her senses. She had to focus all her energy on thinking... breathing.

Even after he withdrew his hand, hers burned. And she couldn't quite clear her mind of the sensory details of her dream—the way those hard calluses had pressed against other parts of her body, the strength of those fingers. The way they'd dug into her hips...and lifted her. Heat pooled in her core at the memory, and she had to grip the back of the chair to steady herself.

She couldn't drag her gaze away from his face, but there was nothing in his eyes to indicate that he'd experienced anything at all when they'd shaken hands. Perhaps those intent gazes they'd exchanged yesterday had been one-sided also.

Good news, she told herself. That was just the way she wanted it. And it was relief she was feeling, not disappointment. Or worse, rejection. She'd had more than her share of that lately.

Plus, she had a job to do.

"...took the liberty of ordering you an iced latte."

"Hmmm?" Naomi interrupted her little self-lecture to glance down at the table and she saw the frosty glass for the first time. Then she carefully settled herself in the chair.

"Tess, the waitress who's been taking very good care of me, said that you have a weakness for caramel-mint flavor."

"Yes, yes, I do," Naomi said. *In addition to my weakness for priests,* she thought a bit giddily. Then she forced herself to meet his eyes again.

Nothing.

Get over it, Naomi. You can still indulge your secret fantasy. The fact that he's as oblivious as Father Bouchard was will make it simpler.

"She's also going to bring out an order of the house scones. They are evidently aware in the kitchen that you didn't order up any breakfast."

He was thoughtful. And kind.

But *thoughtful* was not the word that came to mind when she remembered the man she'd seen wearing nothing but that small, damp towel last night. No, he'd looked like a man who would take what he wanted and damn the consequences. A little thrill moved through her.

As she lifted her glass and took a fortifying sip, her gaze never left his. She couldn't seem to make herself look away. The man had a definite physical pull on her.

"The staff here are all worried about you," he said. "You've been through a rough time."

Understanding was what she read in his eyes now. But she was aware that his hand moved toward hers. Just a matter of an inch or so across the table. He drew it back without touching her.

What would happen if she touched *him?* The temptation to find out flared brightly for an instant before she tamped it down and gripped her latte more tightly.

Focus. Business. "I understand from Avery that you're thinking of using Haworth House to hold some retreats for the purpose of recruiting new seminarians."

"I'm looking to attract larger numbers, and this apears to be a perfect spot for a retreat." He sipped his coffee, then set it down. "Is that why you came here?"

"To retreat?" She frowned. "I'm not sure I like the military connotation of the word."

"To think things through then," he suggested.

"Yes. That's exactly why I came here."

"Is it working?"

Her brows drew together as she considered. "I think so." She thought of the decision she'd made to stop using her tote and borrow Jillian's purse. It was mostly symbolic. Baby steps. "I'm starting to sort things out, decide what I want to do next."

"In a religious sense, retreats are supposed to lead to renewal."

She shifted her gaze to the stretch of blue ocean visible through one of the courtyard's archways. "I've always thought that's what the original owner, Hattie Haworth, found here. I think she came here not because she was running away, but because she wanted to start over."

His hand moved again. She didn't see it this time, but she sensed it, and when she turned to look at him, there was a tension in his shoulders and in the line of his jaw that hadn't been there before.

"Look," he said. "I know I'm a complete stranger. But if you feel the need to talk to someone, I'm a pretty good listener."

He had a nice voice, soothing, sincere. This time she admitted to herself that it *was* disappointment she was feeling. Yesterday, she might have looked for understanding, been happy to find it. Today, it wasn't enough. Impatience rippled through her. Not nearly enough. And as easy as he was to talk to, the last thing she wanted right now was a father-confessor.

She bet Hattie Haworth hadn't wanted one, either. During her movie career, she'd allowed her decisions to be influenced by men—the head of her studio, then her husband. And they'd both dumped her when she'd no longer been of use to them.

The parallels to her own life were blatantly evident.

This time it was more than a ripple of impatience she felt. But she curbed it. There was a part of her that wanted to get up and just walk away. But she had the hotel to think about.

Get the business over with, Naomi. She summoned up a smile for the priest. "What can I tell you that will convince you to bring your potential seminarians to Haworth House?"

He clasped his hands together on the table and leaned forward in his chair. Seconds ticked by as he studied her the same way she'd studied him a few moments ago. For the first time, she saw a hint of the intensity in his eyes she was certain she'd detected during the heated glances they'd shared the day before. And she felt again that ripple of awareness along her nerve endings. Maybe the sexual pull between them hadn't been all one-sided. Maybe he was as attracted as she was—and was trying to cover it.

Wasn't that exactly what she was doing? Hadn't she decided that if she continued her fantasy with him, she would handle it the same way she had at fourteen—like a secret schoolgirl crush?

He opened his mouth, but whatever he might have said was interrupted by Tess as she delivered a platter of hot blueberry scones.

"Can I get you anything else, Father? Ms. Brightman?"

"Thanks, Tess," Naomi said. "We're fine."

With a little salute, the waitress hurried away.

They reached for the scones at the same moment. Their fingers brushed and jerked back, toppling two of the warm delicacies off the pile and onto the ground. They moved together again, scraping back chairs and squatting down to retrieve the fallen scones. When their hands connected this time, he didn't pull his away. Instead, he took her fingers in a firm grip, and she felt a tremor move through her.

They were close, nearly as close as they'd been in her dream when he'd knelt on the edge of her bed. The strength of those fingers, the hardness of his hand, were just as she remembered them. So was the heat that streaked up her arms and shot straight to her center.

Everything else was new—and real. There was the scent of the sea mingling with the tanginess of the blueberries and the more earthy scent of him. She felt each one of his fingers tighten on hers as if he were suddenly determined to keep her there. A wild thrill rippled through her. This wasn't the relaxed, charming man she'd just been having a conversation with. This was the man she'd locked gazes with across the length of the courtyard. Every nerve in her body began to throb.

Their faces were only inches apart. She'd never before been so intensely aware of anyone. The color of his tanned skin, the way his breath feathered over her cheek and along her jawline. But she couldn't look away from his eyes. Fascinated, she watched the blue-gray irises darken until they were only shades lighter than his pupils. It wasn't kindness or understanding she saw now, but something much hotter. Something that made her lose her breath as if she'd just raced to the top of a very high cliff.

He wanted to kiss her. The desire she saw in his eyes triggered a burst of hunger inside of her. She wanted his mouth on hers. Here. Now. All it would take was the tiniest movement and their lips would touch, meld, mate. In one instant, she would become intimate with the shape of his mouth, the taste and the texture of his tongue. Anticipation cut off her thoughts, and every weighty worry she'd carried around for the past two weeks spun away. Greed she hadn't known she was capable of rioted through her. He had to kiss her. She had to know.... "Father."

It was the word, just that one word that allowed Dane to get a thin grip on reality. On control. He never should have touched her. Even though it was the only thing he'd thought of doing since she'd walked across the courtyard to join him. The problem was, she seemed capable of triggering a disconnect between his body and his brain.

Twice he'd caught himself reaching for her hand before those damn scones had fallen. Twice. And he still hadn't released her fingers. Nor could he prevent his gaze from dropping to her mouth.

Her lips were warm, moist, parted. He'd very nearly kissed her. He still could—so easily. All he had to do was close the little distance between then, and he would finally know what she tasted like. And once he tasted her...? If he lacked his usual control now, what would happen then? The fact that he was strongly tempted to damn the consequences and find out finally gave him the strength to release her hand. But he still didn't move.

Who the hell was she that she could have this effect on him? He'd been observing her for two weeks and he'd known he was attracted. But shouldn't there have been some sign, some warning that she was the kind of woman who could tempt a man to throw aside all logic, all intellect?

All thought of his job?

Her eyes were wide, and he could read the innocence as well as the desire. Was that part of what drew him? Mesmerized him? Anger simmered through him. Not at her but at himself. Whatever hold she had on him, he was going to have to figure it out.

"Here, let me help you with those."

They both turned as Tess dropped to her knees and gathered up the scones. Neither of them moved even after Tess had hurried away. Dane noted that it was Naomi who gathered herself first and, using the edge of the table for support, rose to her feet.

His body was still pulsing, his blood pumping when he stood. And he wasn't the only one, he realized when he spotted the pulse hammering at her throat. She was feeling at least something of the turmoil that was brewing inside him. That was some consolation. Not much. If what they were feeling wasn't mutual, it would be a lot easier to handle.

"I'm sure I haven't answered all of your questions yet, Father," Naomi said.

"No," Dane agreed. Not by a long shot.

"I think a tour might be in order." She glanced at her watch. "Unfortunately, I have an errand to run in town this morning. How about I meet you back here around one-thirty and personally show you some of the highlights that Haworth House has to offer? There's one spot along the beach that can't be missed, especially if you're thinking of spiritual reading and meditation."

"Sure."

The smile she gave him was brief, professional, but as she walked back into the hotel, he noted that her gait wasn't quite steady.

His would be, he hoped. In just another few moments. It was only then that her words sunk in. She'd invited him to a private spot on the beach. And he'd agreed to go with her.

Shit.

Would a priest have agreed to do that? Better still, would *he* be able to do that and keep his hands off her? He'd barely restrained himself from kissing her within sight of everyone in the courtyard a few moments ago.

Silently, Dane cursed himself as he drew out his wallet and dropped a bill on the table. What would or would not happen on the beach was the least of his worries right now. She was running an errand in town, and that might prove the perfect opportunity for Davenport to contact her.

5

AVERY HAD BEEN absolutely right about rides in convertibles, Naomi decided as she pulled in to a small municipal parking lot near the pier. A fast drive with the top down had allowed her head to clear. It had also managed to pull all the pins out of her hair. Glancing in the rearview mirror, she studied her reflection and barely recognized herself. Her cheeks were flushed, her hair windblown.

But that was just the tip of the iceberg, she thought as she grabbed the purse she'd borrowed from Jillian and locked the doors. Something had shifted inside of her when she and Father MacFarland knelt to get those fallen scones. When he'd taken her hand and nearly kissed her, she'd recognized the man she'd seen standing below her window in the courtyard. It was as if Dane MacFarland was really two men—the friendly but reserved priest and the sexy man she'd seen last night wearing nothing but a towel.

Perhaps all priests had those two sides to them—the spiritual advisor and the man.

It was the man who'd *nearly* kissed her. And there

was a part of her that was beginning to get tired of nearlys.

On the fast ride from the hotel, she'd had some time to think and she'd reached a conclusion. Limiting the fantasy of seducing Dane MacFarland to her diary and hoping that it might trigger another erotic dream was the way she'd handled her infatuation with Father Bouchard. Good grief! She was nearly twice as old now, and there had to be a more adult solution.

And that was as far as she'd gotten.

Because she wasn't seriously considering making the fantasy a reality. Was she? Pressing a hand against the jitter of nerves in her stomach, Naomi headed across the parking lot. Baby steps, she reminded herself. All she had to do for now was follow Jillian's advice and shop. When she reached the sidewalk, she paused a minute to take in the view.

The pier and the restaurant Avery had taken her to the day before were to her right. A few of the tables on the patio were occupied. Her glance strayed to a man in a large straw fisherman's hat. There was something vaguely familiar about him.

For a moment, she narrowed her eyes and studied him, taking in the worn jeans, the T-shirt with torn-off sleeves, the muscled arms. He held something in the palm of one hand, and as she watched, he lifted it. Sunlight glinted off metal. Some kind of lure, she supposed. Then he casually tipped it from one palm into the other and back again.

Familiarity stirred again. And then it clicked. She'd seen Michael do the same thing. The last date they'd had, he'd played with the key chain he'd given her in the same way. She passed her gaze over the man again, and this time she noted the tattoo on his upper forearm.

Good lord, was she becoming paranoid? The conservative Michael Davenport would never have a tattoo. And a lot of men probably used that same gesture.

Deliberately, she glanced beyond the patio of the restaurant to a sandy curve of public beach crowded with chairs and colorful umbrellas. Gulls cried overhead. Children laughed as they raced through the frothy waves that pushed relentlessly against the shore.

Farther out in the water, a couple of fishermen lounged in small boats, their lines bobbing gently in perfect rhythm with the movement of the waves. As one of their lines dipped, Naomi shaded her eyes and watched the man straighten and begin to let out more line. The back of her neck prickled.

She barely stopped herself from whirling around. Instead, she turned slowly and pretended to casually scan the street to get her bearings. Though his tackle box still sat on a chair, the man with the tattoo was gone.

To her left lay the main street of the town, stretching inland a couple of blocks from the pier. As she crossed the wide, paved street, the few pedestrians strolling along the sidewalk didn't so much as glance her way.

She spotted a bank with a clock tower, a professional office building that housed a real estate office, a law firm and an art gallery. Ahead of her, on the corner, was a coffee shop, Uncommon Grounds, that offered shady sidewalk seating beneath a pretty green-striped awning.

Two customers sat outside. One had his back to her and wore a baseball cap. He dug in the duffel bag in the chair next to him and took out a book. The other man, large and round with a grizzled beard, was scribbling on a folded newspaper. Working a crossword puzzle, she guessed. Neither of the men paid her any attention as she walked past them, and the prickling sensation didn't reoccur.

In the next block up, she saw Book Traders—a bookstore, candy store and touristy gift shop. It was just the kind of place that Michael Davenport would have been drawn to.

Annoyed that she'd let her ex-fiancé intrude on her thoughts once more, she whirled and cut a diagonal path across the street, heading to the boutique Jillian had recommended. Discoveries sat directly across from the coffee shop, and she would have made her way there earlier if it hadn't been for the feeling that she was being watched and her paranoid need to study everyone on the street.

The display window intrigued her immediately. It was free of the usual mannequins. Instead, a silky cloth the color of the sea flowed over tiered shelves and merchandise was artfully arranged on each one. Her eyes were immediately drawn to the lingerie. A lace bra and matching panty in a lemony color lay as if the wearer had just carelessly discarded them. Next to them, other bra-and-panty sets in a rainbow of colors were stacked neatly.

Her own underwear was as practical as the clothes she wore over them. But the bits of frothy lace in the display window were pure fantasy. A sudden image flashed into her mind. She stood on the balcony of her room wearing nothing but the yellow lace bra and panties. Across from her, Father Dane MacFarland stood on his balcony wearing nothing but that skimpy towel. And it was the man who looked at her, not the priest, and even in her imagination that heated gaze made her head spin. For an instant the sensation was so intense that she had to put her hand against the glass to steady herself.

Get a grip, Naomi. A fantasy was one thing, an obsession quite another. Drawing in a deep breath, she ordered herself to focus on the window display. She'd come here to shop.

T-shirts and shorts were arranged closer to the front of the window. There wasn't a neutral color in the bunch. Tucked in a far corner was a small ancient-looking sea chest with a cornucopia of fashion jewelry pouring out of it. Here, too, color seemed to be the order of the day—turquoise, coral, peridot and garnet.

Against a sunny yellow backdrop, two sundresses in splashy prints hung from hangers. One had a halter top, the other spaghetti straps with little bows. Beneath each sat strappy sandals in a coordinating color. Naomi glanced down at her sensible black shoes with medium heels.

Definitely drab.

As she stepped into the interior of the dress shop, she stopped and blinked, recalling that moment in *The Wizard of Oz* when Dorothy's world went from black and white to Technicolor.

A petite woman with short brown hair and the face of a pixie hurried out from behind a cash register, her hand extended. "Hi, I'm Molly Pepperman. Welcome to Discoveries."

Naomi took the offered hand. "I'm Naomi Brightman. I believe you've met my sister Jillian."

Molly's face lit up. "Indeed, I have. She said you might stop by. You can browse to your heart's content. Or you can put me to work. When I was a little girl, I wanted to grow up to dress the stars for the red carpet."

"I think I should put you to work. Not for any red carpet. But I'm in desperate need of a complete wardrobe makeover."

The woman rubbed her hands together, beaming. "You've just made my day."

Naomi glanced around the store. It was a large space, but in spite of the variety of the inventory, it didn't appear crowded. "Where do we start?"

"At the foundation, naturally," Molly said. "But first we're going to take a little tour of the store and you can let me know what catches your eye. A dress, a color, a bracelet. Anything."

Naomi frowned. "A fashion sense is not my strongest suit."

"Let me worry about that." Molly grabbed a basket. "Think of it as being in a grocery store. You just tell me what you like."

Naomi took another look around. "What about those sunglasses?"

"Excellent choice. Very Jackie O."

The fact that Molly hadn't laughed, or worse, snorted at the fact that her first choice had been sunglasses, made Naomi straighten her shoulders. "On second thought, I don't want them."

"Okay."

She met Molly's eyes. "Sunglasses are for hiding and I'm through with that."

Molly beamed a smile at her. "Then you've come to the right place. What else strikes your fancy?"

Naomi swept her gaze around the store. She could do this. "The very first thing that caught my eye was the matching bra and panties in the window—the yellow ones."

"And you claim you have no fashion sense. Those

are just in." Molly urged her toward the front of the store, pulled the backdrop aside and scooped up the lingerie.

"I like the blue ones, too."

"Who wouldn't?"

As Molly added them to the basket, Naomi again experienced the prickling sensation at the back of her neck. She snapped her head up and scanned the street in front of her. The coffee shop was kitty-corner to Discoveries and one of the men she'd seen earlier was gone. The other appeared to be totally focused on his crossword puzzle.

"Anything else while we're in the window?"

Naomi turned back to the display. "The turquoise print sundress and sandals."

"They're my favorite, too." Molly added the sandals to her basket and slipped the sundress off its hanger. "We'll worry about sizes later."

After they'd walked through the entire store, Naomi watched as Molly unpacked her basket and hung everything outside a small dressing room.

"What do you think?"

What she thought was that nothing she'd chosen looked anything like the old Naomi Brightman. "In Boston, I would have had to run the gamut of a mall to put all of this together. And I probably wouldn't have had the courage to buy any of it. How do you manage to offer such a wide range in a small store?"

"My great-grandmother opened this space as Pepperman's General Store back in the thirties. So we've always stocked a variety of products. When I came back here after graduating from fashion school in New York, I talked my grandmother into letting me make some changes. Now we only cater to women—or to men who want to shop for women."

"What should I start with?" Naomi asked.

"The bra and panties. I know they'll fit so go ahead and try them on. I promise, it will make all the difference. Once you get those on, I'll hand you something else."

Naomi stepped into the dressing room, closed the door and studied herself as she began to slip off her clothes one piece at a time, folding each garment carefully and putting it on a nearby bench. She wished it were going to be just as easy to discard old habits, old ways of thinking.

Once she'd slipped into the lemon-colored bra and panties, she appraised herself in the mirror. There was definitely something…different about her. Stepping closer, she tried to figure it out. The garments were thin and transparent. As she turned to one side, then the other, she felt the slight scratch of the lace against her skin and her nipples. Her whole body tingled with heightened awareness.

It was the same face, the same body. But not quite…

"What do you think?" Molly asked through the door.

"I look like me."

"But…"

"I don't feel like me." She traced her fingers along the lace that left the top of her breasts bare and then ran them down her sides to where the edge of the bikini stopped high on her thighs. "I feel sexier."

Molly's laugh drifted over the top of the dressing room door. "What else?"

Naomi remembered seeing the lingerie lying discarded on the rippling blue silk in the display window. The bra and panties had looked as if someone had just stripped out of them and tossed them aside. And the fantasy that had been teasing at the edge of her mind ever since blossomed.

Closing her eyes to picture it more clearly, she once more imagined that she was at the window of her balcony just as she had been the night before. Across the courtyard, Dane MacFarland stood at his phone with nothing but the damp towel hitched low at his waist.

Only this time when he turned and his eyes locked on hers, she did more than stare back. She stepped out into full view on her balcony. Though she hadn't thought it possible, his gaze seemed to grow more intense. Then with her eyes steady on his, she lifted her hands and unhooked the bra. The sensation of the lacy fabric sliding down her arms and breasts was enhanced by the searing heat of his eyes as he followed its progress.

Trembling now, she hooked her thumbs into the waistband of the panties and pushed them slowly down her hips. Fire and ice shimmered along her nerve endings as the panties slipped to the floor.

When he stepped onto his balcony, the intensity of the pull she felt had her moving closer to the mirror. Dizzy with desire, she swayed and flattened her palms against it to remain upright. Then she leaned her forehead against the coolness of the glass.

"Naomi?"

"Yes," she managed to reply. With great effort, she opened her eyes. She was back in the dressing room, and the lemon-colored lace lay at her feet.

"They've done research on why women wear sexy underwear—whether it's for the men in their lives or for themselves," Molly said. "And they discovered that the majority of women wear sexy lingerie for themselves."

Naomi gave her reflection a sideways glance. Not entirely true. From first glance, the sexy undergarments had triggered thoughts of a man. One man.

"I'll bet you that if you put that business suit back on, you won't see yourself in the same way. And you won't feel the same way."

She already felt different. The old Naomi hadn't ever fantasized about stripping for a man. She'd certainly never done it in real life. And it wasn't just any man she was imagining herself getting naked for. It was a priest.

Guilt and pleasure flooded her, making her fumble as she refastened the bra. "I'm going to take these in every color you've got."

"Done."

"Now hand me the sundress and the shoes."

Molly opened the door and passed them in. "One question."

"Sure."

"I want to know who the lucky man is."

Naomi pulled the sundress over her head. It was the one with the spaghetti straps. The material had no sooner settled into place than she imagined herself untying one of the straps and then the other. "How do you know there is a man?"

"You have a look in your eye. Is it seduction or revenge?"

"Maybe a little of both," Naomi said as she stepped into the sandals. She studied herself in the mirror. The reflection was a far cry from the woman who'd stepped into the dressing room in that dull business suit.

And maybe this didn't have to do with a man at all.

Maybe it was high time she did something just for herself. And her fantasies about stripping for Dane MacFarland? Well, she still had time to sort that out.

DANE SHIFTED UNCOMFORTABLY in his seat. The hardon had been with him ever since he'd seen Naomi and the petite brunette take two sets of lingerie out of the display window. To top it off, since she'd abruptly left the courtyard that morning, he felt he'd been playing catch-up. And it was his own damn fault. He'd spooked her when he'd taken her hand and come close to kissing her. Hell, he'd spooked himself.

Following her into the village hadn't gone as smoothly as he'd hoped. His rental car couldn't match the speed of the Corvette. But thanks to Tess, he had a good idea where Naomi intended to run her errand—a boutique called Discoveries that Jillian Brightman recommended to everyone.

When he'd seen her pull in to the municipal parking lot, he'd parked on a side street. But she was fast. By the time he'd switched T-shirts and donned a baseball cap from his duffel, she'd been headed his way. He'd barely had time to note that Discoveries only had two doors, the one on the main thoroughfare and a side door for deliveries on the cross street. Hurriedly, he'd chosen one of the outside tables at the coffee shop. Although he'd angled his chair away from her, he'd felt her eyes on him and held his breath until she'd crossed the street to window-shop. Only then had he taken a second to strategically assess his surroundings.

Tailing someone in a small village posed problems. The position of the coffee shop in the center of the small shopping district gave him a good vantage point. When she'd finally entered the store, he'd moved inside the shop to a window table that provided more cover.

He could still see her car in the parking lot and Discoveries was across the street. So he'd had front row seating for the articles of clothing she'd selected from the window.

Ever since he'd seen the saleswoman lift the scraps of lingerie, he'd had a tantalizing image in his mind of Naomi wearing nothing but that froth of lemon-colored lace. And during the course of drinking two cups of iced coffee, the image had spun more than one fantasy.

They all began the same way—with Naomi standing in one of those dressing rooms with a three-way mirror. He stood behind her, pulling her against him and tracing his fingers along the top of that lace, once, twice. Then he moved his fingers lower, slowly circling her nipples through the silky fabric before he continued his exploration of the smooth skin that stretched taut over her ribs, becoming unbearably soft as his hands moved lower. And lower.

The first time he'd played the fantasy through, he gripped her hips, holding her close as he slipped his fingers beneath the lace and into her. Keeping his gaze on hers, he drew his fingers out and pushed them in, again and again.

He kept the rhythm slow at first while he read her response from her reflections in the three-way mirror. He caught every nuance—the beat of her pulse at her throat, the catch of her breath, the stiffening of her body when she was almost ready to climax. Each time she neared her release, he stilled the movement of his fingers and held her tightly against him to keep her there, just on the brink of her climax.

Only when she said his name, Dane, did he finally increase the rhythm until she rose up on her toes and arched against him. Then he used his mouth and teeth on the side of her neck until she'd ridden out her release.

And that was fantasy number one. In fantasy number two, he used only his mouth on her. Which had resulted in his current uncomfortable situation.

Pushing the tantalizing images firmly out of his mind, Dane took a sip of his iced coffee and sat very still. He didn't dare move. Thinking of the variety of ways he could give Naomi a climax in the confines of that damn dressing room had aroused him to the point that the slightest shift in pressure against his penis might bring him to his own release.

Not to mention that the more he fantasized about making love to Naomi Brightman, the harder it was going to be to control his desire the next time he was with her.

Time to get his mind off the dressing room.

A glance at his watch confirmed that she'd been in the boutique for almost an hour. And that was out of character for her. Two weeks he'd watched her in Boston, and he'd never seen her shop for a thing except a few groceries and her morning lattes. In spite of the pleasurable side trips he'd imaginatively taken into Naomi's dressing room, he hadn't seen anyone go into Discoveries either through the main or side door.

So if Michael Davenport was planning to make contact with her in Belle Bay, he probably wasn't going to do it in the boutique. But something told him—a gut instinct he'd learned to trust—that Davenport was keeping an eye on her. The question was, where would he make his move? And when?

Dane scanned the area outside the window of the coffee shop. The tables under the awning had filled. None of the customers bore any resemblance to Davenport. And only one man had been there as long as Dane had—the large round man with the grizzled beard who'd been focused on his crossword puzzle.

Shifting his attention back to the street, Dane noted that the pedestrian traffic had thinned to a few strollers the next block up and a couple of delivery trucks were slowing the flow of traffic from the pier.

A flutter of movement across the street caught his eye. Naomi appeared in the open doorway of the boutique, her purse slung over her arm and both hands occupied with shopping bags. For a moment, he simply stared.

The short-skirted sundress was a far cry from the conservative suit she'd been wearing that morning. And her legs were, well…they seemed to go forever.

He was trying to stop staring at them when the small brunette he'd seen earlier gave her a quick hug. As they chatted, the man with the grizzled beard dropped a bill on his table and strode toward the corner. He crossed the street in the direction of Discoveries, and as Naomi started toward the pier, he fell into step about twenty paces behind her. They were the only two people on the sidewalk.

Coincidence? Hard to accept that when his senses had shot to full alert. On the other hand, his senses seemed to be on full alert 24/7 when it came to Naomi.

In Boston, he hadn't been the only one watching her. Why would he be the only one here?

But if Grizzled Beard was a Fed, he ought to be better at his job. He shouldn't be getting as close as he was.

Letting his instincts rule, Dane chucked the baseball cap into his duffel and strode out of the coffee shop.

By the time he'd cleared the sidewalk tables, Naomi was a block away, and the man following her was less than three stores behind her.

A hell of a lot closer than Dane was.

He thought of calling out to her. But there was still that slim possibility he was overreacting. Highly probable when he'd been overreacting to her on so many other levels.

Instead, he picked up his pace until he was parallel to her on his side of the street.

A plan formed in his mind. She was no doubt on her way to stow her purchased items in the Corvette. As soon as she did, he'd call out to her and cross the street. The fact that she wasn't alone might scare off the man following her. It wasn't a bad plan. He was about to put it into action when two large delivery trucks groaned to a stop, totally blocking his view. Dane moved faster. As he did, he glanced over at the pier, and an abrupt movement caught his attention.

A man wearing a straw hat shot up from one of the patio tables and leaned over the railing. Dane might not have noticed if his view of Naomi hadn't been temporarily blocked. And even then he might have dismissed the man as a curious onlooker if the fisherman's hat hadn't fallen off and dropped to the pavement below.

Recognition punched into him with the impact of a fist. Michael Davenport. The man's gaze was riveted on whatever was happening on the other side of the street. Dane gauged the distance. Thirty seconds tops and he could be at the restaurant. He'd have the scumbag in his hands.

He bolted forward, and then he heard the scream.

Naomi.

Heart pounding, Dane turned on a dime, shot into the street and made an end run around the delivery truck.

And then she screamed again.

6

"HAVE FUN!" Molly followed Naomi into the bright sunshine and then hugged her.

"I intend to." Because her arms were completely occupied with shopping bags, Naomi settled for kissing her new best friend on the cheek.

"You sure you don't need help to your car?" Molly asked. "I could lock up the store for a few minutes. Heck, I could close for the rest of the day after the sale you've given me."

Naomi laughed. "I'll be fine. My car is just down the street." She was almost more grateful for the laughter she'd shared with Molly over the past hour than she was for the new wardrobe. Almost.

"Come back soon," Molly said.

"I will." And she was going to do more than come back. If she weren't so hamstrung by the fact that any communication with her sisters had to be kept to a minimum, she would have called Jillian and Reese right away. At some point during the myriad of outfits she'd tried on, it had occurred to her that the hotel might very well benefit from a small branch of Discoveries opening up at Haworth House. Both businesses could profit from the exposure.

She was picturing it in her mind when she experienced that same prickling sensation she'd had earlier when she'd first walked past the coffee shop.

This time, it was more than annoyance that streamed through her, and she didn't bother to hide her reaction. Whirling around, she spotted the large round man with the grizzled beard she'd seen earlier. He didn't look like any of the Feds who'd tailed her in Boston. But the moment she'd turned to face him, he'd shifted his gaze to the side, and he hadn't slackened his pace. A guilty reaction if she'd ever seen one. He was less than twenty feet away and closing the distance between them quickly.

Naomi considered her options. She could continue on her way and ignore him. She could make a run for her car. Or she could stay right where she was.

Hadn't she decided that she was done with allowing any man to manipulate her?

"Are you following me?" she asked.

Startled surprise flickered over the man's face before his eyes met hers. Then he raised both arms and lunged toward her.

Acting purely on instinct, she waited, sidestepping him at the last minute. He plowed forward into thin air, and she sprinted back in the direction of Discoveries.

Behind her, she heard a man swear. A horn blared on the street, and she battled to find traction on the sidewalk in the new sandals she wore.

A hard shove from behind sent her into a skid on a collision course with a brick wall. At the last second, a hard tug on the strap of her purse stopped her momentum and spun her around.

"Give me the purse, lady."

Naomi dropped her shopping bags and gripped the strap of her purse with both hands. "Get your own."

He pulled and she lunged forward.

"Give it up."

"I don't give up," she said through gritted teeth.

He pulled and she slid forward again. This couldn't be good for her new shoes.

"The purse belongs to my sister so you can't have it," she said.

This time he gave the purse a quick jerk and she lost her balance, tumbling into him. It was his turn to stumble backward. As they both teetered wildly, Naomi seized the opportunity to loop the strap of the purse a second time around her wrist.

His face was red now, he was taller by at least six inches, and his eyes had darkened with anger. "Dammit, lady. Give me the damn purse."

"No."

In a lightning-fast move, he dropped the strap and clamped a large hand on her arm. "Then you can come along with it."

For the first time, fear sprinted through her. She dug in her heels. Or at least she tried. But the new sandals merely skidded along the sidewalk. Naomi screamed.

The man started to run. On the side street ahead, the door of a dark-colored sedan opened. Panic slithered up her spine. She was running now, too. Nothing she did seemed to curb their forward momentum. Screaming again, Naomi swung the purse full force into her companion's face.

It was his turn to holler as he dropped her arm and covered his nose with his hands. She stumbled sideways into a wall and used it to regain her balance. Blood oozed from between his fingers. Using both hands this time, she whacked him in the face again.

Howling, he sprinted toward the waiting car, and she raced after him. She was gaining on him when strong hands closed around her shoulders and lifted her up. Her feet dangled inches from the ground.

"Are you all right?"

"Stop him! He's getting away!"

It was only when she was on her feet and able to turn around that Naomi recognized her rescuer. "Father MacFarland? What—"

"Did he hurt you?"

"I'm fine." She turned back in time to see the would-be purse-snatcher shove aside an elderly couple and dive through the open door of the sedan. Tires squealed as the car shot away from the curb and up the side street.

Craning her neck, she caught the license plate. "VGB 1370."

"What?" he asked.

She met his eyes. "VGB 1370. That's his license plate number. That man just tried to steal my purse. I'm going to report him and his license plate to the sheriff."

"I've got Sheriff Kirby right here."

Dane turned to see the small brunette from the boutique hurrying toward them, her cell phone clutched in one hand. At her side, taking one step to her two, was a tall man with blond hair. He wore khaki trousers and a matching short-sleeved shirt. A gun and a badge were clipped to his belt.

Thanks to Ian's research, Dane knew that a Kirby had been sheriff on Belle Island for the last four generations, and Nate Kirby had taken over for his father three years ago.

A few curious people had begun to gather, and Dane

joined them on the sidelines as Naomi described what had happened and the sheriff took notes. Dane needed a moment to regroup. Hell, he needed several to get her scream out of his head and to tamp down on the mix of emotions he'd felt. Fear had been at the forefront, but guilt and a fierce need to protect her had been racing right behind.

So much for the emotional distance that was essential to getting Davenport and keeping Naomi safe.

Davenport was no longer on that patio. He'd checked that out while Naomi was getting the license plate. In front of him, she had emptied the contents of her small purse into Molly's hands—car keys, a wallet, a pen and a notepad from the hotel, a lipstick. The sheriff had opened the wallet, and Dane was close enough to see there was very little cash and only a couple of credit cards.

As Nate took her through what had happened again, Dane paid closer attention and replayed the scenes in his mind. Thanks to the delivery truck and his distraction with Davenport, he'd missed a lot of it. But what he'd seen had been enough to have fear icing his veins. By the time he'd spotted her, Grizzled Beard was dragging her toward the corner. The stalled traffic in the street had slowed Dane down, and panic had knotted in his belly when he'd realized that he wasn't going to make it to her in time.

Then she'd whacked the guy in the face with her purse.

A part of him had wanted to cheer when she'd slammed it into him a second time. But when she took off after him, he'd wanted to shake her. If he hadn't reached her in time to stop her, there was no telling how the tussle might have ended. The guy might have grabbed her again. She could have been hurt. Worse, she could have been in that car and speeding out of town.

He was still frowning at Naomi when the sheriff approached him and introduced himself.

"Nate Kirby. And you're Father MacFarland."

At Dane's raised brow, he continued, "Any new guest at Haworth House feeds the gossip mills here on Belle Island for at least a few days." He flipped his notebook to a fresh page. "I'd like to get your take on what happened."

Dane met the sheriff's eyes. "My take is that Ms. Brightman is a very lucky young woman."

"We can agree on that. Good thing you were in the vicinity. Where were you exactly?"

Dane turned to look at Naomi. With Molly's help, she was gathering up her packages. "I've been in the coffee shop for the past hour or so."

"How well do you know Ms. Brightman?"

Dane glanced at the sheriff. "I met her this morning at breakfast up at the hotel. I'd asked the manager for a meeting with the owner because I'm thinking of using the hotel facilities for a possible retreat."

"Are you aware of her troubles in Boston?" Nate asked.

"As a matter of fact, I am. Her face has been on the news quite a bit over the past few weeks. You think this might have some connection to that?"

"I'm not big on coincidences," Nate said.

Dane wasn't, either.

"Ms. Brightman says that she spotted her attacker at the coffee shop earlier. He was at an outside table working a crossword puzzle. She thought at first he might have been a Federal agent sent here to keep tabs on her. Did you happen to notice him?"

"Yes, I did. When I arrived, there were only a few customers."

Nate Kirby turned to look up the street. "Not a bad place to pick if you wanted to keep someone under surveillance."

For a moment, Dane said nothing. Did the sheriff suspect that *he* had used the coffee shop to keep an eye on Naomi? Finally, he said, "Or if you were biding your time, waiting for the right moment to snatch her purse."

"Ah, yes, the purse." Nate closed his notebook and tucked it into his pocket. "We don't get a lot of street crime in Belle Bay. But this one appears to have been planned."

Well planned, Dane thought. And very nearly successful.

"Did you get a look at the driver of the car?" Nate asked.

"No. I was a little preoccupied keeping Ms. Brightman from running after it." Truth told, he'd been too focused on Naomi all morning. And it had caused him to second-guess his instincts.

"You're running the license plate?" Dane asked.

"Tim, my deputy, is checking it out. It's from a rental agency here on the island." Nate glanced at Dane. "It'll probably be a dead end."

Dane thought so, too. But Ian might have better luck than the local police.

When Naomi dropped one of her shopping bags, he shifted his gaze to her and frowned again. Her hand was visibly shaking as she reached for it. He moved toward her, took her arm with one hand and then lifted the shopping bags. He glanced back at Nate. "The adrenaline rush is wearing off. I'm going to drive her back to the hotel."

"Good plan. I'll be in touch."

"Me, too," Molly said with a wave.

"I'm fine," Naomi muttered when they reached the parking lot.

"You will be." When he heard the hint of sharpness in his tone, Dane drew in a deep breath and let it out. He'd better remember who he was supposed to be. Father MacFarland. Good listener. Confessor. Confidant. New best friend.

When they reached the Corvette, he removed his hand from her arm and held it out for the car keys. Then he watched carefully as she retrieved them. As she did, he got an even closer look at the purse. It was small, about seven inches by four, and it folded to snap at the top like an envelope. It was a lot smaller than the huge tote she'd carried around for the entire time he'd had her under surveillance. What had happened to it? he wondered. But it wasn't a question Father MacFarland could ask.

"Here." She dropped the keys into his hand.

"Good girl," he murmured.

Her eyes flew to his. "No way. That was the old Naomi Brightman. She was the good girl."

Tilting his head to one side, he studied her for a moment. There was a martial light in her eyes that he hadn't seen before. "I was referring to the fact that your hands aren't trembling anymore."

She held them out in front of her, noted that they were steady. "Oh."

"I still think I should drive." After stowing the shopping bags and his duffel in the trunk, he escorted her to the passenger side and opened the door. "Of course, my motives are somewhat suspect. Priests don't get a lot of chances to drive a Corvette."

Instead of climbing in, she leaned against the side of the car and met his eyes. "I'm sorry."

"Because I don't get to drive fast convertibles?"

"No." The corners of her mouth twitched. "I haven't thanked you for what you did back there."

"I didn't do much. It looked to me as though you had the situation under control."

She folded her arms across her chest. "I was just so mad."

Dane's mouth curved. "I got that much."

"I really wanted to hurt that man. Badly. If you hadn't come along, I might have done some real damage."

"Or gotten hurt pretty badly yourself. He was a big guy. And he wanted your purse. In spite of the double whammy you delivered, he might have rallied and taken you with him."

She waved a hand. "That was not going to happen. The purse belongs to Jillian. I didn't even ask her if I could borrow it. Not that she would mind. My borrowing it, I mean. She definitely would have minded the man stealing it."

"Why did you borrow it?" Dane kept his tone casual, mildly curious.

She waved a hand again. "I decided I wanted—I needed—a change, and I didn't want to lug that tote around anymore. The purse is a symbol. Little steps."

"Little steps?" Dane asked.

"It's a way to ease into making a change in your life. You know, one step at a time. The big tote I carry around is a kind of talisman for me. It's Prada. My sisters gave it to me when I left for college, and it cost them a fortune. I've used it ever since."

"Would you have let the thief take your tote?" Dane asked.

Her brow furrowed for a moment. "Good question. A week ago, maybe. Not today. Not anymore—ever."

Pushing herself away from the car, she paced a few feet and whirled to face him again. "It wasn't just about the purse. When I turned and saw him heading toward me, it was the last straw. I've had some...problems lately. And I'd felt I was being watched earlier before I went into Discoveries. So I just couldn't let that man push me around. It was time for me to take a stand. Can you understand that?"

"I think so. You've had a rough time lately, lots of pressure." Not to mention the betrayal, the heartbreak. "I'd say you've been handling things pretty well."

Her eyes narrowed. "You know about the Boston stuff."

"Priests watch CNN and read the newspapers. It's easy enough to understand how you might use the jerk who tried to snatch your purse as a scapegoat."

"Scapegoat." She spoke the word as if she were testing it. "Yes, I suppose that's what I did. Except usually scapegoats are more innocent than he was. In addition to being a symbol for the people who have been giving me a lot of grief, he also wanted to steal my purse. He deserved a good smack in the face."

"True enough."

She frowned. "But I'm not usually like that."

"Like what?"

She waved a hand. "I felt like some kind of avenging angel."

It was as good a description as any, Dane thought. Standing there in the parking lot, with her hair a tumble of red and gold and the strap of her sundress falling off one shoulder, she exuded a kind of valor he might have associated with Joan of Arc.

Without thinking, he moved forward and adjusted the strap of the sundress. The instant his fingers brushed against her skin, he couldn't resist the temptation to close his hand over her shoulder. A sensation of torrid, liquid heat ran through him, and his focus narrowed to her. Only her.

Everything else spun away—the Corvette, the parking lot, the noise of passersby on the street. All he knew was the quick hitch of her breath, the pulse quickening at her throat, and the way her eyes had darkened to a deep sea-green, the kind a man could drown in. Willingly. Flashes of the fantasies he'd entertained in the coffee shop filled his mind, making it too easy—much too easy—to forget that he shouldn't be touching her. That he couldn't pull her close and satisfy the edgy need that raged inside of him each time he saw her.

Naomi couldn't think at all. The searing intensity she saw in Dane's eyes blocked out reason, logic, words. All she could do was feel the panicked excitement prickling along her nerve endings, the brutal pounding of her heart against her chest, the burning of her lungs as the air grew too thick to breathe.

All she could see was him standing so close that his heat enveloped her. And his scent—something musky—had her head spinning, her bones melting. Her whole body yearned for him with a hunger she'd never known before. When she swayed, his hands gripped her upper arms and pulled her close. For one heady moment, she felt what it was like to have every hard angle of his body pressed against hers. Each contact point set off dozens of explosions of pleasure. Her skin was still vibrating with the shocks when the blaring horn of the noon ferry blasted the air.

Just as quickly as he'd pulled her close, he set her away. The jarring sense of loss was so acute that it took a moment for reality to trickle in. The second long blast of the ferry's horn helped. By the time it faded, Naomi could hear the laughter of passersby, the noise of a car backfiring. She found she was leaning against the fender of the car. Good thing because she couldn't feel her legs.

"Are you all right?" Dane asked.

She nodded, not certain that her voice would work yet. And if it did, she couldn't be sure that she wouldn't beg him to touch her again and to…what? To make love to her right there in a public parking lot in the middle of Belle Bay?

He said nothing more but merely opened the passenger door and waited for her to climb in. She did, grateful that her body was once more connected to her brain. Then he walked around the car and slid in behind the wheel.

Still throbbing, she studied his profile as he drove the Corvette out of the parking lot. She wanted to ask him if he'd felt any part of what she'd felt in that brief contact. Were his thoughts still swimming as hers were? Was his body still pulsing with wild, urgent needs?

And what were they going to do about it? That's the question that kept her head spinning as he drove them out of Belle Bay.

CAREFUL TO KEEP his simmering anger on a tight leash, Michael Davenport stowed his fishing pole and tackle box and climbed into his car. Things were not going as smoothly as he'd expected.

And they should have been. Up until now, everything had unfolded the way he'd known it would. Naomi had taken her first opportunity to flee Boston and come to Belle Island. And she'd brought the money.

All he had to do now was bide his time until the perfect opportunity presented itself to take back from her what belonged to him. He'd been sure that today might be his lucky day when he'd happened to overhear a snatch of conversation between two of the hotel staff. Mr. Cooper's Corvette was to be brought around at ten-thirty sharp because Ms. Brightman was driving into the village.

He'd quickly stowed his hedge clippers into his duffel and slipped away. His plan had been to reach the village before she did and then wait for the right time to approach her.

It would be risky, but not nearly as risky as trying to make any kind of move on her at the hotel. Once in Belle Bay, he'd chosen to wait for her at the small café on the end of the pier where she'd lunched the previous day with Avery Cooper. From his vantage point, he hadn't had the best view of the small drama that had unfolded two blocks away. But he'd seen enough to know that it had been more Keystone Cops than *Mission: Impossible.*

But they'd nearly gotten Naomi's purse. And that had given him a few very bad moments. He was almost sure that she didn't have what he wanted in it. But still...if she had...

When the anger surged, he drew in a calming breath. The man who'd pressured him into a partnership was no doubt behind the totally mishandled snatch-and-grab.

He was a bungler, and he would pay for this. Michael started his car and pulled out of his parking space.

On the upside, he'd now learned two things about his partner. The man knew more than Michael had previously thought, and he was becoming more and more of a loose cannon.

The little problem of his partner could be dealt with—would be dealt with, he thought as he left the village. He knew how to handle troublesome partners.

What had disturbed him more was the difference in Naomi between yesterday and today. There'd been something about her earlier when she'd arrived in Belle Bay in the red Corvette. It wasn't just the windblown hair. It was the way she'd walked. And the purse—it wasn't the one she always carried. That was totally out of character. Then there was that unexpected moment when she'd noticed him at the table on the patio.

He was confident that his disguise had held. But he didn't like the fact that her attention had been drawn to him in the first place.

Even more disturbing was the woman who'd stepped out of the small boutique up the street. She was a sharp right turn from the Naomi Brightman he'd dated for the past six months. The clothes were part of it, he supposed. But not all.

Definitely, not all.

And that was another complication.

Most of his success in the past had been based on his ability to read people. But the Termagant who'd struggled with the would-be purse snatcher and bloodied his nose didn't mesh at all with the woman he'd known.

Dammit. He slammed his hand down hard on the steering wheel. Thanks to his stupid partner and Naomi, he was going to have to speed up his plan. And speed often led to mistakes.

He'd have to be very careful not to make one. There was too much at stake.

His frown deepened as the car began to climb the long hill to the hotel. The priest also bothered him. The man had looked vaguely familiar, but he hadn't been able to place him. That didn't bother him as much as the fact that the cleric had just been too Johnny-on-the-spot. And he'd appeared out of nowhere.

There were bound to be people watching Naomi, hoping that he would contact her. A priest would make a very good cover.

His cell phone rang as he rounded the curve and headed toward the employee parking lot of Haworth House.

"Well," the voice said.

"The men you hired didn't get Naomi's purse."

There were two beats of silence on the other end of the line. "What are you talking about?"

Michael laughed. "I'm talking about the failed snatch-and-grab that has all of Belle Bay talking. I watched the whole fiasco from the pier. Ms. Brightman nearly cleaned your guy's clock. Luckily, your two goons managed to get away. If they hadn't, they might be talking to the local sheriff right now. And blabbing about who hired them. I hope you were discreet."

This time the silence was longer and gave Davenport a great deal of satisfaction.

"Even if your purse theft had been successful, you wouldn't have gotten the money. All that risk for nothing."

"You're lying."

"I know just where the money is. If you want to see any of it, you'll let me do this my way."

Another beat of silence.

"So what's *your* plan?" his unhappy partner asked.

He laughed again into the phone. "I have several. But it would be better if I didn't have to worry about extra players." Then he hung up.

He still had time. And he was close to Naomi. He could get to her whenever he wanted to.

7

THE MOMENT THAT Dane MacFarland pulled to a stop in front of Haworth House, Avery Cooper ran down the front steps. "Are you all right?" He drew Naomi out of the car, then held her at arm's length to study her. "He didn't hurt you?" He turned to Dane. "Nate said you were there, Father, that you intervened."

"She was doing all right on her own," Dane said.

"I'm fine." It was the truth as far as her scuffle with the purse was involved. She hadn't thought of it at all on the fast ride up the hill to the hotel. Dane and what had happened in the parking lot had pushed the incident right out of her mind. "How did you hear about it so quickly?"

"This is Belle Island." Avery frowned and shook his head. "Purses don't get snatched here."

She lifted her chin. "No, they don't. At least not from me."

Avery drew her into a hard hug. "That's my girl. C'mon in. I'll order you some tea or brandy. Or champagne to celebrate the obvious success of your shopping spree."

Good grief, she'd pushed the new clothes out of her mind, too. Naomi managed a smile. "I'll pass on the drinks. I'm going to unpack all the stuff I bought."

As Avery drew her up the steps, she felt her brain cells begin to click. Distance. That was the key. If she could just keep away from Dane for a while, she could figure everything out and decide what she was going to do.

"We have an appointment at one-thirty."

Dane's words had her whirling around on the top step to face him. The bottom dropped out of her stomach, and she felt that immediate pull so strongly that, if Avery hadn't been holding her arm, she might have run right back down to him.

He was wearing sunglasses so she couldn't see his eyes, couldn't tell if he was the priest or the man. Her gaze lowered to his mouth. That belonged to the man, and she wanted it pressed against hers. He was still standing on the other side of the Corvette, but even at that distance, she could almost taste it, almost feel it close over hers.

Desperately, she tried to push the outrageously tempting thought away. But she couldn't stop the torrid rush of heat that flooded her senses.

If she could taste him, just once, maybe she could be free.

He walked around the car, lifted her shopping bags out and handed them to a waiting staff member. Then as he climbed the steps, he met her eyes again. "Unless you'd rather postpone…"

Distance, she reminded herself. Taking Dane Mac-Farland for a walk along a private beach wasn't going to provide that. It was much more likely to get her… "I'll meet you here at one-thirty."

He nodded. "See you then."

Naomi kept her eyes on him until he disappeared into the lobby of the hotel.

"I could take him off your hands," Avery said. "I know every spot the island has to offer. Then you could rest."

Rest? She wasn't sure she would ever rest again. Not until… "No, I'll take him."

A dark, guilty thrill moved through her at the thought of doing just that.

Avery tipped up her chin and studied her face. "You're up to something, sugar."

"No." She felt the heat rise in her face and she pressed a hand against the nerves jittering in her stomach. "Maybe…I don't know." She couldn't actually be thinking of doing…what she was thinking. "Absolutely not."

"Right." Avery slung an arm around her shoulder and gave her a friendly squeeze. "I've been there and done that more times than I can count. I'll have the kitchen pack you a lunch for your little beach excursion."

"CALL ME AS SOON AS you get anything on that license plate, Ian," Dane said. He'd phoned his brother the moment he'd reached his room. "And if you get a name we can use, one that belongs to a real person, I'd like to know who hired them."

"Will do. You sound worried."

"Davenport is in town."

"You saw him?"

"For a split second. My attention was divided because Naomi was being stalked by the guy who tried to snatch the purse." And if he hadn't been convinced that

Naomi was in danger, he might have gotten his hands on Davenport.

"Did he recognize you?" Ian asked.

"I doubt it. Three years ago in Kansas City our meeting was very brief, and I was wearing a disguise."

"And he thought he'd killed you along with his partner."

"Yeah." Dane pressed a hand against the small bullet scar on his lower back from his last encounter with Davenport. "So even if he thought I looked familiar, he's unlikely to make the connection." He'd been lucky that day. And thanks to him, Davenport's partner hadn't. He'd been the one who'd convinced her to set a trap.

The same thing was not going to happen to Naomi.

"Well, it's good news that he's there," Ian said. "That means you were right. She must have something he wants. All you have to do is wait."

"Yeah." Trouble was, there were other things he wanted to do while he waited. Distracting things. Dane ran a hand through his hair as he strode to the window and drew the curtains tight. If he didn't block out the view of Naomi's balcony, chances were very good that like sixteen-year-old Romeo Montague, he'd be tempted to watch for her to appear.

And he needed to think. More and more he was finding that impossible to do when he was close to her. Talking to his brother was helping him refocus on the job. Turning away from temptation, he strode back to the foot of the bed and sat down.

"Davenport was probably behind the purse snatching," Dane said. "He had a ringside seat." Dane thought of what he'd seen—the way Davenport had shot up from the chair. In his opinion, the guy had been trying to get a closer look at the disturbance on the street like everyone else on the patio. "Not even the sheriff here thinks that the purse-snatching incident was a coincidence. The question is what does it mean?"

"Well, let's see."

In his mind, Dane pictured his younger brother leaning back in his chair, perching his feet carefully next to his computer screen, then crossing his legs.

"I'm not the trained field agent, but if we're operating on the theory that Naomi has something he wants…"

"Go on," Dane said. He'd given it some thought on the drive back to the hotel. Concentrating on the possible ramifications of the attempted purse snatching had helped him overcome the urge he'd had to just take Naomi away from Belle Island.

He didn't understand it. And definitely didn't like it. The woman had started pulling at him the first time he'd read her file. Now it was as if she had some kind of control over him—the kind a puppeteer might have over her marionette.

It went far beyond the physical attraction he felt for her, although that was strong enough. That moment in the parking lot when he'd pulled her against him, she'd dragged him in so deeply with that soft, pliant body, that fragrant scent. He'd begun to drown in her, eagerly, with no thought of swimming to the surface. And even when he'd summoned up the strength to release her, something inside of him had taken a little tumble.

Not good.

"I'd say whatever it is has to be small enough to fit in her purse," Ian said. "Like a safe-deposit key or a locker key."

Dane shifted to lie back on the bed. "Or something else that's small but worth a lot of money. A rare jewel, coin, stamp—something that would fit with what he did three years ago. That time he converted his ill-gotten gains into a priceless bronze figurine."

"Any chance the two thugs were after more than the purse?"

"Such as?"

"Her."

"I didn't see the whole thing, but Naomi claims the guy only started dragging her toward the car when she wouldn't part with the purse. Plus, if Davenport or his buddies wanted to snatch her, there are more efficient ways to do it."

"How?" Ian asked.

"I would have parked the getaway car at the side of the boutique and gone in through the delivery entrance. Then I would have taken care of the shop owner and escorted Naomi out into my car. Less than two minutes from start to finish. Out on the street, there's always the risk of someone interfering. I think their goal was the purse."

"And if Davenport was behind this, he thought he could get it without making actual contact with her. This failure may force him to change his plan."

"And that could put Naomi Brightman in mortal danger."

"You, too," Ian pointed out. "Let's not forget Kansas City. The man doesn't like his plans messed with."

Dane's glance shifted back to the closed curtains. "On another topic—you dig up anything at Our Lady of Solace boarding school that might explain why Naomi thought she recognized me?"

"Still working on it. Want me to fly over there?"

Dane laughed. "You *are* desperate for a little field work. Give the license plate priority over the boarding school."

As he ended the call, Dane stared at the ceiling. Davenport hadn't made the move he'd expected, which would make it harder for Dane to predict the next one.

But he didn't doubt for a minute that the man would go to great lengths to get the money he'd embezzled. He thought of the woman he'd tailed in Boston for the past two weeks, someone on the conservative side, someone predictable. The avenging angel who'd smacked that thug in the face was anything but predictable.

And if Michael Davenport couldn't predict what she would do, Naomi was in even greater danger.

Dane needed more than ever to become her confidant and find out what she knew. And he had to protect her. He'd slipped up in Belle Bay. And in Kansas City three years ago, he hadn't managed to protect anyone. Not even himself.

As a priest, he couldn't—he shouldn't—touch her.

Problem was, couldn't's and shouldn'ts weren't having their usual effect on him. His growing desire for her had the power to block out all other priorities. Adding to the problem was the fact that he wasn't just physically attracted to her. He liked her. And each time he saw her, that liking grew.

He'd learned the hard way to be a realist. His family had been taken from him, and he'd made himself accept the fact that it would take time to reunite everyone. The reality here was two-pronged: he had a job, one he wasn't going to walk away from, and he wanted Naomi Brightman more than he'd wanted any other woman.

He looked toward the balcony window again. Bottom line, priest or not, Dane wasn't sure how much longer he could go without touching her. Every inch of her.

And more.

NAOMI FASTENED HER EARRING, then gave herself a last once-over in the mirror. She'd tried on three outfits before finally settling on the simplest one—a pair of white shorts, a red halter top Molly had insisted she buy and red sandals.

She'd felt compelled to run up to the tower room to view herself in Hattie's mirror. Now, fisting her hands on her hips, she glanced around the room that had once been Hattie's private boudoir and ultimately her reinvention space. She was here. Somewhere. Naomi could sense it. "Look, I could use some advice. And not just about the clothes."

She spoke in a hushed voice, and the only response to her question was the distant sound of the sea.

What had she expected? But she'd felt the need to talk to…someone. Not Avery. He was a man, and as understanding and supportive as he was, she was used to talking to women. Her sisters.

Naomi turned back to study her image in the beveled glass again. "I can't really talk to Reese and Jillian about this…this priest thing. They'd be shocked. And I'm still the older sister. The role model. How can I tell them about my secret fantasy to seduce a priest? The one I drew out of your hatbox."

In the distance, the sound of the sea seemed to grow louder.

"I figured if anyone would understand, you would."

How many times had the aging ex-Hollywood star stood right here and examined herself in this very glass? For a moment, Naomi thought she detected something in the mirror—a flicker of light? She couldn't see anything when she stepped forward, but the room grew a little colder, and she experienced a deepening of the connection she'd felt from the beginning with the island and with Hattie Haworth.

Encouraged, she said, "In less than half an hour, I'm going to the beach with Father Dane MacFarland. And I want him so much that I can't think straight." She clasped her hands in front of her, determined to get it all out. "When I'm with him, all I can do is feel. It's... wonderful. Amazing." So amazing that she couldn't prevent herself from doing one quick spin. As she did, the outfit she wore caught her eye. The shorts and halter top were such a sharp contrast to her regular clothing. The sundress she'd worn when she'd left the shop had made her feel feminine. But this... "He makes me feel like a woman."

Had she ever felt like a woman before? Big sister? Yes. Confidante? Often. Friend? Absolutely. Attorney? She thought of all the dull, quiet suits, the days she'd spent in the firm's law library, the tedious time spent in court, sitting second chair to her boss.

Turning, she glanced around the room again. "The avenging angel role is easier." She waved her hand back and forth. "Whack, whack, and you're done. Being a woman is more complicated."

Nerves jittered again in her stomach. Turning to focus on her image again, she willed them to settle. "Is that how you saw yourself when you looked in this mirror, Hattie? Was it here that you first saw yourself as a woman?"

Deep in the glass, a light shimmered.

Naomi started, then forced herself to continue. "Yesterday when I got here, I decided to become the new Naomi. My plan was to take little steps. But what I'm thinking of doing is taking a flying leap. With no safety net. I'm not sure that I'll have the guts to do it. But if I go to the beach with Father MacFarland, I don't think I'll have a choice." Her hands were so tightly clasped now that her fingers were going numb. She lifted her chin. "I'm actually thinking of seducing a priest."

There. She'd said it aloud. Nerves had tightened in her stomach, but lightning hadn't struck her. Then something stirred in the air around her, and Naomi peered more closely into the mirror.

The light shimmered again—just for an instant.

"Did you actually seduce a priest, Hattie?" she whispered. "Have you ever wanted anyone so much that you would break all the rules? Commit the biggest sin?"

This time there was no shimmer of light. The sound of the sea was the only answer she heard. A sudden thought struck her. "Or maybe all those parchments in the hatbox are just 'let's pretend' fantasies—like the sex games they publish every few months in *Cosmo*."

Whirling, she paced away from the mirror, then turned and strode back to face it again. "You've probably never read *Cosmo*, but this isn't a make-believe fantasy. It's not a game. I'm involved in the real deal here. He's a priest, and I can't stop myself from wanting him. I'm thinking of committing a big sin. *Huge*. And it packs a double whammy because if I do go ahead with this, I'm dragging him into it just the way Eve dragged Adam."

Naomi paused. She was beginning to babble. To a ghost. Pressing a hand to her stomach, she stepped closer to the mirror. Did she really think that by coming here she could reach a decision? If she'd had a choice, hadn't it already been made?

If she went to that beach with Father Dane Mac-

Farland... The only question remaining was how in the world did one go about seducing a priest?

Her stomach felt tense and her palms went damp. She wasn't sure how long she stood there gazing into the mirror before the glimmer of an idea came to her. Of course. Heart pounding, she placed a hand against the glass. "Thanks, Hattie."

Then she ran out of the tower room.

8

DANE WAS LEANING against the Corvette when Naomi raced down the steps of the hotel. For a moment all he could do was stare. He even forgot to breathe.

She was stunning. He'd known she was attractive in a subtle way. And he'd imagined her in various stages of nakedness. But it was a far different experience to see her in the flesh.

And there was definitely a lot of flesh showing. His eyes never strayed from her as Avery loaded a canvas tote into the back of the car. And when she turned to take the keys from the hotel manager, Dane let his gaze travel down her nape over her shoulder blades and the smooth, generously exposed back to her waist.

Oh, yeah, there was more than enough flesh. Any benefit from his cold shower was completely negated once he allowed himself to look at her legs. Now all he could think of was having them wrapped around him, trapping him as he pounded into her.

He was grateful for the support of the car. His palms were pressed flat against the fender, and they burned.

Not from the heat of the sun on the metal, but from the overwhelming need to touch her.

"Ready?" she asked.

More than, Dane thought as he nodded.

"Let's go then." She moved to the driver's side and climbed in.

"Right." He folded himself into the passenger seat. Knowing that he was in big trouble, he fingered the Roman collar as she shot the car out of the hotel driveway.

SWEAT TRICKLED DOWN his back as Michael Davenport watched them drive off. Posing as one of the gardening team provided a good cover, but trimming hedges in a maze that seemed at times to be as large as Canada was damn hard work. Plus, he was limited to watching comings and goings. The upside was that the tedious and repetitious job had allowed him to work off some of his anger and clear his head.

And his patience had finally paid off. Stepping into the shade at the side of the hotel, he set down his clippers and took a long swallow from the thermos that hung from a strap on his shoulder. The tote bag the hotel manager had placed in the back of the Corvette had picnic lunch written all over it. That meant the priest and Naomi would be absent from their rooms for a time.

It was a double bonus as far as he was concerned. If the priest was FBI, then that meant there'd be one less set of eyes looking for him. And Naomi would be out of her room for at least an hour or two. That would give him time to look around. If he found what he was after, he'd take it and leave. If not, he'd at least have an opportunity to plant some surveillance equipment in her rooms as well as the priest's. One way or another, he'd have what he needed soon.

It wasn't an ideal situation. Feds usually traveled in pairs. But one was easier to handle than two. And he could handle himself. The closest call he'd ever had was in Kansas City three years ago. Everything had gone smoothly as usual. But when he'd shown up for that final meeting with his partner, she'd had someone with her.

He'd shot the man before he'd even had a chance to turn around. Then he'd had the chance to see the expression on his partner's face before he shot her.

Both of them had paid for the betrayal. And his current partner would pay also.

The anticipation of that happening had Michael's lips curving as he bent down to open his duffel. After exchanging his baseball cap for the fishing hat he'd worn in town and packing up his clippers, he headed for the back entrance of the hotel.

He was due for a change in luck, so there was a chance that he'd find what he was looking for in Naomi's room. If not, he wouldn't be that disappointed. His favorite part of every con he worked was the challenge of the endgame.

SHE DROVE AS SHE HAD on the way into Belle Bay earlier—fast, with just a hint of recklessness. Dane kept his eyes on the road, putting his hand up to the dashboard only once when she careened around a curve and braked to an abrupt stop to avoid a collision with a cow.

"Sorry," she said. "The car seems to set my inner speed demon free."

"No problem." This was the side he hadn't seen in

Boston. He risked a quick sideways glance. She was smiling as she sent the car speeding up a hill, then took a quick turn onto a dirt road. Had the recklessness been there all along, just waiting for the right moment to spring free?

"You said you watch CNN and read the newspapers, Father. Do you ever watch movies?"

Grateful for the distraction of conversation, Dane said, "Sure. I've been known to do that."

"What kinds?"

"Old ones. The kind they run all night long on free movie channels." Those were the only ones he'd had access to while he was growing up.

She sent him a surprised look. "Then you've probably seen some of Alfred Hitchcock's films?"

"All of them. My favorite is *Rear Window.*"

"This drive reminds me of *To Catch a Thief.*"

"The wild ride that Grace Kelly takes Cary Grant on in the hills above Monaco."

"Exactly." She slowed as she took the next curve, then eased the car to the side of the road and parked. "What do you think?"

What he thought was that he'd better stop thinking that Grace Kelly's motivation on that drive was to seduce Cary Grant. Some distance below them was a stretch of sandy beach trapped between two cliffs. Falling away from the cliffs were huge piles of rocks that extended about a quarter of a mile out into the sea. Waves slapped against them, sending spray high into the air. But the water trapped between the rocks formed a small cove with quiet blue water. From their current position, the outline of Haworth House could be seen to their left, and to their right, on an angle of land that jutted out into the sea, sat a lighthouse. "It's beautiful. And so quiet."

The sound of the surf that he could hear so clearly at the hotel and at the busy pier in town was muted. The only things marring the silence were the steady sound of the wind and the lonely cry of a gull as it soared into the sky.

"We have to climb down," she explained. "It's a little steep at times." She shot him a glance. "Are you okay with that?"

"I'll manage." The more important question was how he was going to handle things once they were on that deserted beach.

"The land belongs to the hotel, so the locals don't come here. And I advised my sisters against advertising it to the guests." She made a sweeping gesture. "When the tide comes in, the rocks on either side become very slippery, and the beach completely disappears. A couple of the caves nearly fill with water. No one comes here. It's very private."

Keep your mind on the job, MacFarland.

As she spoke, she got out of the car and grabbed a small straw bag from the backseat. "Can you get the other tote? Avery had the kitchen pack us a picnic lunch."

Dane lifted out the canvas bag and followed her to the edge of the cliff. The land sloped down gradually for a while in terraced ledges. Here and there, wildflowers pushed their way out of crevices in the rocks. But it was Naomi's scent that wrapped around him, teasing his senses.

"This way." She started down.

Dane glanced over his shoulder before he followed. There was no one in sight. This area of the island

seemed entirely isolated. That meant they were probably safe from Michael Davenport. That was the good
news. The bad news was that Naomi might not be safe
from him.

When one of her sandals set off a shower of stones,
he stepped around her and took the lead. There was
a path of sorts, and at times, it was wide enough that
they could walk side by side. But the narrowness of the
walkway caused occasional contact, and he was very
much aware of each brush of her arm against his.

"Do you mind a personal question, Father?"

He shot her a sideways glance, but her focus was on
the path. "No."

"Do you have to wear that collar all the time?"

"No."

"Why are you wearing it here at Haworth House?"

As a reminder, he thought. "Because I'm here on
priest's business, and I'm sold on this place. Especially
this beach. I think it's the perfect spot for meditation
and prayer."

This time it was his foot that dislodged a shower of
stones, probably punishment from on high for the lie.
When she gripped his arm, he felt the imprint of each
one of her fingers. "We should walk single file for a
bit," she said. He was careful not to meet her gaze as
he stepped into the lead.

Naomi found herself looking at his back. He'd slipped
completely into priest mode, the man she'd been talking
to at breakfast before the scones dropped. But she was
looking at the body that had fascinated her from across
the courtyard last night. Up close and personal. He'd
changed into a gray cotton T-shirt that hugged a narrow
waist and stretched tight over broad shoulders. Above
the neckline, the Roman collar was just visible.

"Why did you become a priest?"

There was a beat of silence before he said, "Because I wanted to make a difference. I wanted to help people. Why did you become a lawyer?"

Naomi frowned as she moved to walk beside him again. He'd had to think about it. Surely it was a question he'd answered many times. And he'd countered with another question. That was an age-old method of avoidance. "I became an attorney so that I could protect my sisters."

As they reached a curve, he glanced at her. "I can understand that."

There was something in his eyes. Regret? Pain? "You have family?"

"Yes." This time the silence stretched for two beats. Overhead, a gull gave a lonely call.

"I lost them."

"Lost them?" She put a hand out and rested it on his arm. "How awful."

He turned and glanced down at her hand, but he didn't draw away. "I don't know why I said that. I never talk about it."

"Maybe you should. What happened?"

He turned away then and began to walk. Naomi was pretty sure he wasn't going to say any more. If her throat hadn't been so tight, she might have assured him that it was all right if he didn't want to talk about it.

"My mom was what you might call nontraditional in her approach to child rearing. She loved us, but she also liked men, a lot of different men. When I was old enough to think about her behavior in a more analytical way, I came to the conclusion that she was looking for Mr. Right and not having much luck finding him. But she never gave up. My two brothers, my sister and I probably all had different fathers. I was the oldest, and when I was nine, she didn't come home one night."

Naomi gripped his arm again. "What happened?"

He shrugged. "I didn't find out until the next morning when the police and social services showed up. She'd been taken to an emergency room where she'd died of a burst aneurysm in her brain."

Something squeezed around Naomi's heart. She pictured him as a nine-year-old trying to make sense of what had happened. She'd been younger when her father had left her sister and her with the nuns and later when they'd received the news that he'd died in a car crash. But she had some idea of the piercing sense of loss, of disorientation.

"I tried my best to keep us together. But I was nine. We had a few days together in a facility before they split us up. I can still see the way my two brothers and my sister looked at me when they were led away."

She tightened her grip on his arm and waited until he stopped and met her eyes. "When my father died, at least my sisters and I weren't alone. My mother was French, and she'd died six months earlier of leukemia. Neither of my parents had any other family, so Dad brought us to this Catholic French boarding school where my mother had gone. Just temporarily until he could make arrangements. He was on his way back to us when his car ran off the road near Monte Carlo. But we had the nuns, and there was never any talk of separating us."

"Like yours, my mother didn't have any family, so I went into foster care. My brother Ian went into a different foster home and he was eventually adopted. My sister, Brianna, was two, and she was adopted. So was my four-year-old brother, Caleb. Sealed records. I'm still trying to locate the two younger ones. But I found Ian.

He was working in research and analysis at the CIA. He's brilliant at what he does, and eventually, we'll find the others."

"I'm so sorry. If there's anything I can do to help...I don't know what I would have done if I'd been separated from my sisters."

He laid a hand over the one that still rested on his arm. "You may have your sisters, but you've suffered losses, too."

She frowned at him. "I lost a job and a fiancé. I didn't lose family."

"Still, it had to be a blow to lose your fiancé. You must have loved him."

"No." Michael had said those words, but she never had. "I thought I loved him. Even after everything I'd learned about him, I still thought maybe I did. I kept trying to put together the Michael Davenport I knew with the man the FBI described to me. The man I became engaged to was thoughtful, kind, very romantic. He was always buying me little souvenirs to commemorate everything that happened between us."

"Like what?"

"Silly things. A key chain, a refrigerator magnet, a little snow globe. I saved all of them. I kept them on a shelf in my apartment. I even brought them here with me. Don't ask me why."

He didn't, but the silence finally made her say, "Probably because I was stupidly trying to hold on to the myth that he loved me. No one had ever treated me with that kind of meticulous attention before. It was very seductive."

"And he was a good lover?"

A mix of surprise and shock rippled through her. She opened her mouth, not exactly sure what she was going to say when he said, "I'm sorry. That was an abominably rude question and none of my business."

She met his eyes directly. "I don't know what kind of a lover Michael would have been. He never did more than kiss me." She felt the rush of heat to her face. "You're probably wondering why I ever agreed to the engagement." She was beginning to wonder, too. "But Michael seemed to be the kind of man a girl *should* fall in love with. He was charming, thoughtful, my boss loved him. I went with the flow." She lifted her chin. "I'm not proud of that."

"Do you think he was in love with you?"

Naomi considered. "He said he was. He acted as if he was. But since I don't really know him, I can't say."

"In my experience, people get engaged for two reasons, love or money. If it wasn't a compelling issue of love at first sight, a man like that, a swindler, must have seen some advantage in establishing a relationship with you. What did you bring to the table?"

She stared at him. "Nothing."

"Don't underestimate yourself."

The sharp impatience in his voice made her blink. She had time to recognize that it wasn't the priest she was talking to now, but before she could say a word, he hurried on. "For one thing, you brought a reputation for honesty. How many clients did he gain access to in the past six months with you standing at his side?"

Surprise rippled through her again, and her picture of her relationship with Michael shifted just as sharply and drastically as if she were viewing it through a kaleidoscope.

Anger surged. "Because of me, he was able to convince my boss and most of our law firm's biggest clients to invest with him. That's why Leo King said he had to let me go. He said he didn't believe that I had anything to do with Michael's schemes, but because it appeared that way, the firm couldn't be associated with me anymore. Michael Davenport used me. I'm not going to let any man do that to me again. Ever."

Afterward, Dane wasn't quite sure how it happened. Maybe it was the mix of emotions that ran through him at her words or the Joan-of-Arc look that was back on her face. Or it could have been that he'd finally given in to the steadily strengthening temptation she'd presented each time she'd touched him on their walk down the cliff. But suddenly she was in his arms, and each delicate curve of her body was pressed against his.

Her eyes widened and darkened immediately. Her breath hitched, and the pulse at her throat kicked into that wild rhythm that never failed to trigger an instant response in him.

At first he didn't move. When she wrapped her arms around his neck and he felt that strong, supple body vibrate against his, he pulled her even closer. The priest should have stepped back. The man simply couldn't.

He'd never known a desire this raw, this reckless. He wanted her, needed her the way a man needed to eat after a long fast—the way a man might crave air after a long time underwater. Once again the world spun away until all he knew was her. He leaned forward, closing the distance so that he could finally taste her when he felt the collar around his neck cut into his skin.

Reality thundered back into place, abruptly widening the scope of his world. He was here to do a job. And the woman in his arms might be in mortal danger. He wasn't sure which of those concerns gave him the strength to loosen his hold on her.

"I can't, Naomi. We can't." Gripping her wrists, he removed them from around his neck.

Her eyes were still cloudy with desire, but he didn't miss the flash of pain before she averted her gaze. "Because you're a priest."

It wasn't a question so he was saved from having to make an answer. Good thing. He was certain the lie would have choked him. As it was, it took all his concentration not to reach out to her. Her vulnerability pulled at him. But if he touched her again…he wouldn't be able to stop.

It took her only a moment to gather herself, and she moved past him to take the lead again. Admiration streamed through him. In addition to all her other qualities, Naomi Brightman had more than her share of true grit.

She didn't speak until they reached the beach. "Hungry?"

"I could eat." The moment had passed. She wasn't going to bring it up again. But Dane was very aware it wasn't relief he was feeling as they walked toward the water.

With her eyes firmly fixed on the sea, she sat down, slipped out of her sandals and slid her feet into the warm sand. He allowed himself a long look at those legs before he dropped down beside her. Then he busied himself with unpacking a thermos and plastic cups. By the time he'd poured drinks and screwed the cups into the sand, she'd extracted two Chinese take-out containers. "It's my sister Reese's idea to pack picnic lunches this way. It cuts down on sand."

Dane opened the container she passed him, found two sandwich wraps and handed her one.

"I hope you like chicken curry," she said.

"If it tastes as good as it smells, I do." He bit into the wrap, but in spite of the explosion of flavors on his tongue, he was still wondering what Naomi would taste like.

For the next few minutes, they ate their way through the sandwiches in silence. Dane tried to regroup. He'd have had a better shot if he hadn't sat down so close to her. She was less than a foot away. On top of that, the setting itself was weaving its seductive magic. It offered privacy and the illusion that whatever happened here could stay here. And it didn't help one bit that each wave that crashed into the shore had him replaying in his mind the scene in *From Here to Eternity* when Burt Lancaster and Deborah Kerr made love with the surf thundering around them.

Pushing the image firmly out of his mind, he attempted to shift his focus back to the job. Davenport was here on the island. And he was making plans. That was what he had to remember.

Out of the corner of his eye, he watched her repack the picnic tote. When she drew her knees up and wrapped her arms around them, her legs didn't brush against his, but some of the sand her movement displaced did, and he felt a little jolt. She might just as well have touched him. He'd never in his life been so sensually aware of a woman. How far would she take him when he kissed her, when he touched her, really touched her? He wanted to run his hands over her, mold every inch of her.

What in the hell was wrong with him? He wasn't a teenager with raging hormones. Wise decision or not, he was here alone with her and he had the perfect opportunity to persuade her to open up. He needed as much information as he could get on Davenport if he was going to have any chance of predicting the man's next move.

"What do you think of this place for a retreat, Father?"

He turned to her. It was the first time since they'd reached the beach that he'd met her eyes. Her breath caught and he watched a tremor move through her.

He knew exactly what she was thinking. Their minds were running down the same path at breakneck speed, and if he didn't keep his foot on the brake… He raised a hand to finger his collar as a reminder. "It's perfect. I could see doing a morning prayer service here while the sun is rising."

Prayer service. Glancing away, Naomi tried to picture it in her mind. And failed. All she'd been able to think about since they'd sat down in the sand was the scene from *The Thornbirds* movie in which Father Ralph had chased Meggie across the sand and finally trapped her beneath him. Only it hadn't been Richard Chamberlain and Rachel Ward she'd been picturing. It had been Dane and her.

It could so easily *be* her lying beneath Dane in the shallows. As the images played out in her mind, she'd felt the ebb and flow of sand and shells beneath her back and the much faster rhythm she was creating as she matched the movements of Dane inside of her.

Turning, she studied him as he sat facing the sea, leaning back on his palms, his long legs stretched out in front of him. They were close, their arms almost touching, and his were covered with hair. She knew that he had hair on his chest, too. What would it feel like against her palms? Against her breasts?

Everything inside of her yearned to know. And wasn't that desperate desire for knowledge the ultimate temptation? It had cost Adam and Eve Eden. And if she sat here another second, she was going to climb right on top of him.

Only to be rejected again? No, to get to the man, she would have to deal with the priest first.

And she would. She'd thought of something in Hattie's tower room. She just had to get away from him for a moment to bring it back to mind. Pushing to her feet, she walked on unsteady legs to the edge of the water.

Dane stood as well, telling himself he was glad that she'd moved. Another few moments and his control would have shredded. She would have been beneath him on the sand and he would have been experiencing that first thrust. Her slick heat would have closed around him, capturing him.

He stopped short when he realized that he'd followed her to the edge of the sea. Stuffing his hands in his pockets, he said, "I'm going to walk along the water for a while." He didn't wait for a response. He didn't trust himself. He had to get away. He had to think.

He headed in the direction of the farthest pile of rocks and concentrated on clearing his mind of her. If he acted on what he was feeling, how did that make him any better than Michael Davenport?

Dammit, she'd gotten to him. He never talked about the breakup of his family. He didn't like revisiting those days or recalling how little he'd been able to do to help his brothers and sister.

And that wasn't what he should be thinking about now. He needed to focus on what he'd learned from her. The money Davenport had swindled out of his investors had to be hidden in one of the little mementoes the man had given to Naomi as a romantic gesture.

And Davenport had the advantage there. He knew

which one was worth the jackpot, and because he'd known Naomi for six months, he might also have a good idea where to look for it. But there hadn't been any little souvenir-like trinket in the contents of her purse that morning. Had Davenport expected her to be carrying it with her?

"Hey, wait up."

Dane turned to find that he'd outpaced Naomi by almost ten feet. As he watched her approach, anger surged through him again. How could Davenport have been around her for six months and not touched her? Not had her?

His gaze dropped to her mouth. Even at this distance, he could all but taste her. Desire crept into him, slowly and surely pushing out everything else—the threat, the money, his determination to bring Davenport to justice.

Perhaps if he could have her just once, the ache would go away. In spite of the risk, he could almost convince himself that if he made love to her, he could be free.

"You're angry," she said as she reached him.

He had been a few seconds ago. At himself, because he was coming to loathe what he was doing. What he still had to do. He still needed more information from her. And the clock was ticking.

He managed a smile. "I'm upset with myself because I'm taking up your time when you're under a lot of pressure. And you've been patient enough to listen to my life's story. Maybe I could at least return the favor. I'm a very good listener."

He saw something in her eyes. Annoyance? Impatience? Then both were gone and what remained was that martial light he'd glimpsed earlier that morning in the parking lot.

"Actually, you can help me out, Father. I didn't bring you here strictly on Haworth House business. I also brought you here for personal reasons. I've been feeling very guilty, and I want you to hear my confession."

Dane stared at her. What in the world could Naomi Brightman want to confess to him?

9

"YOU WANT ME TO HEAR your confession?"

"Yes." She glanced around. "It's very private here. I thought it would be the perfect place."

The wind had picked up enough to push her hair across her face. She tucked the loose strands behind her ear, wishing she could settle her nerves just as easily. "Maybe we could find a more sheltered place to sit."

Leading the way, she chose a wide flat rock. Its position behind a boulder gave them some protection from the breeze blowing in off the water. They sat next to each other, not touching, and Naomi folded her hands in her lap in the same way she had many times when she'd gone to confession. But this time she clasped them together to keep them from trembling. Then she turned slightly to face him.

"Anything I tell you is protected by the seal of confession, right?"

"Yes." His gaze searched her face. "Does this have something to do with Michael Davenport?"

It was concern she read in his face, and that was so *not* what she wanted to see. "This has to do with me."

She'd had quite enough of Michael influencing her life. She was never going back to the old Naomi who would let herself be used as a pawn. Or who would take no or "we can't" for an answer.

"Go ahead then," Dane said.

Naomi drew in a deep breath and let it out. "I'm attracted to you. I was from the first moment I saw you." When he opened his mouth, she held up a hand. "And that's just for starters, Father. I also know that you're attracted to me. Am I right?"

"Yes."

Just that one word set her pulse pounding. But even if he hadn't admitted it out loud, the concern in his eyes had changed to something hotter and much more reckless.

"But—" he began.

She held up her hand again. "I'm not finished with my confession. If you interrupt me, I might not get it all out."

This time he merely nodded his head.

"I was attracted to you when I saw you standing in the courtyard. Then I saw the Roman collar. Discovering that you were a priest—for most women that should have been the end of it. He's a priest. Vow of celibacy. Hands off."

He hadn't moved. Neither of them had since they'd sat down. But his eyes had grown even darker, and tension radiated off him in waves.

Her heart was pounding so loud that she could hear it above the noise of the surf. "When I learned you were a priest, I only wanted you more." She unfolded her hands long enough to wave one of them. "You're going to say it has to do with the whole forbidden-fruit thing. But it's more than that."

Then she told him everything about her crush on Father Bouchard and the fantasies she'd created in her mind and in her diaries.

When she finished, he said, "Why have you told me all this, Naomi? If you want absolution, you haven't done anything wrong."

Lifting her chin, she locked her gaze on his. "I've certainly entertained some very impure thoughts."

"You haven't acted on them."

"Not yet." She rose, paced a few steps away, then turned to walk back. "I want to act on them. I'm not fourteen anymore. And I'm not willing to relegate what I'm feeling for you to the world of fantasy. I want to make love with you."

There. She'd said it. When he opened his mouth, fear and panic bubbled up inside of her. He couldn't say no. She simply wasn't going to let him. "Hear me out."

She felt as if she were in court arguing the most important case of her career. Except she was winging it. "I'm improvising here. Usually I have a plan that I've worked on for days. I always know exactly what to do next. With you it's different." She strode toward him. "I know it's a bad thing I'm asking you to do. I know I'm trying to tempt you into sin. But I'm tired of being a role model. Fed up with being someone's pawn."

Realizing that she was on the brink of babbling again, she pulled herself back. "This is the first thing I want to do for myself. So if lightning doesn't strike me dead, I have a proposition for you. I just want to make love with you once."

When she paused, he said nothing. But what she saw in his eyes had her heart leaping and her throat going bone dry. "I can promise you discretion. No one will ever have to know. And there are no strings attached.

You can cancel your plans for using Haworth House, leave, and we never have—"

The rest of her sentence faded when he rose and took one step to close the distance between them.

"Can I speak now?"

Panic bubbled up again. This was it. He'd say no, and she'd have to come up with Plan B. And C if need be. She sent up a little plea to Hattie that she'd figure them out. Then she nodded at Dane.

"You had me at 'I want to make love to you.'"

"I did?" Surprise and disbelief led the feelings that flooded her. The confession strategy had worked. Should she have known it would be that easy?

When he framed her face with his hands, everything else faded in the heated pleasure of his touch, in the anticipation of what was to come. If his fingers hadn't been holding her up, she would have simply melted into the sand.

Dane didn't say anything else for a moment. He was surprised that he'd been as articulate as he had. Any brain cells still in working order had started to click off the instant she'd said that she was attracted to him.

There was something very powerful about words, and he'd told her nothing less than the truth. Once she'd given voice to the words *I want you,* he'd known that he wouldn't leave the beach without having her. The story of her adolescent crush on the French priest had worked on him, too. He'd actually felt a flash of jealousy, and the one coherent thought that had registered in his mind was that if anyone was going to fulfill her fantasy, it was him.

He traced her lips with the pad of his thumb. "I hope you don't regret this, Naomi."

"I won't." She put her hands on his shoulders, rose on her toes. "I hope you don't, either."

He would. But the regrets would come later. For now, he had this time with her. And his only thought was to make it count.

Her arms were already around him, pulling him closer. "Kiss me."

He lowered his mouth to hers. He thought he was prepared. After all, he'd spent a lot of time imagining what it would be like to kiss her. But he found himself in uncharted territory. They were standing well away from the shore, but the instant they were mouth-to-mouth, he could have sworn the sand shifted under his feet. He was certain the sound of the waves grew in volume until it thundered around them.

Her taste—he couldn't seem to get enough of it. He'd expected sweetness, and there was a layer of that. But as her tongue tangled with his, he discovered a banquet of other flavors—heat and spice and something darker that lingered just out of reach. He dove deeper, dragging her with him until he was drowning in her.

Her surrender. He'd lain awake nights dreaming about it, but he hadn't imagined the intensity of her response, the greedy, avid way her tongue danced with his, seeking, searching, demanding. The way her fingers plunged into his hair or the way she was trying to crawl up his body.

More.

Naomi wasn't sure who said it. But she wanted to scream it as she shoved her hands into his hair. Someone moaned as she dragged him closer. She felt her breasts yield against the hardness of his chest, and a compelling urgency took control of her. This was more than hunger; it bordered on obsession. She wanted nothing but him. Only him.

A gull screamed overhead. Then suddenly, he grasped her wrists, pulled them from around his neck and stepped back from her.

Naomi stared at him. When she tried to step forward, she found that his grip on her wrists allowed him to keep her at arm's length. "Kiss me again."

"I will." He was breathing as hard as she was. "I'm just giving us an intermission. If we're only going to have this one time together, I want to make it count."

"Count?" Staring at him, still overwhelmed by the heat and the needs he'd aroused, she was having trouble focusing.

"You told me that you had fantasies about making love to the French priest—Bouchard. I want to know if you had any fantasies about making love to me."

Fantasies? All she could think of was that anything, everything she'd imagined was becoming a pale shadow of what he'd just begun to show her.

"Did you?" he asked.

"Yes. Why?"

"I thought we could act them out."

"Couldn't we just improvise?"

His lips curved a little. "We'll get to that. But first tell me about your fantasy? What did you imagine me doing to you?"

Her eyes narrowed. "What I imagined was you doing me." Hard, fast, now.

"We'll get to that, too. But I want to stretch out the time we have together. Tell me what else you created in your fantasy."

His idea was beginning to make sense. Perhaps the synapses in her brain were reconnecting. The one thing that she could agree with was that she did want to spin out the time they had.

Since it was all they'd ever have.

"When I was in the dressing room at Discoveries this morning, I thought about stripping for you."

He released her wrists, backed up a few steps and sat down on the flat rock ledge. "Why don't you do that for me?"

She considered for a moment. Clearly, he had more control than she did. He hadn't kissed her on their climb down the cliff face, and he'd been able to back off just now. She wouldn't have objected if he'd just thrown her to the ground and taken her. What would it take to make him lose control?

She raised her hands, tucked the loose strands of hair behind her ears. Then, keeping her eyes on his, she slowly pulled the string on her halter top. In the confines of the dressing room, she'd played to herself. She hadn't been able to fully imagine what it would feel like to have a man watching her while she took off her clothes.

To have Dane MacFarland watching her.

Slowly, she lowered the red halter top, inch by inch. When she slipped it down to reveal her breasts, the heat of his gaze seared her nipples and she felt them harden in response. Encouraged, she let the top pool at her waist, then raised her hands to cup her breasts and lift them. "What if I told you that I imagined you in the dressing room, touching me like this?"

"I'd say that my fantasy was running pretty much in line with yours."

"How about this?" Knowing that he was watching her every movement, she pinched first one nipple and then the other between her thumb and forefinger. His groan brought more pleasure than the way she was touching herself.

"You're more beautiful than I imagined."

The words were nearly enough to break her concentration, more than enough to have her fingers trembling as she ran them lightly down her torso to the red shirt at her waist. She tugged it down over the shorts, then with a wiggle let it slide to the sand. Her fingers fumbled with the snap of her shorts.

"Need some help with those?"

Meeting his eyes, she shot out a hand. "No. The whole idea of a striptease is that you can watch but you can't touch."

"Those are the rules? Sorry, I haven't had a lot of experience with strippers."

"If you're such an old movie buff, you must have seen *Gypsy.*"

The struggle she was having with her shorts was sorely tempting Dane to put an end to the little fantasy he'd requested.

"Besides, it was your idea to stretch out the time."

She had him there. In fact she had him completely. He hadn't expected how tantalizing the stripping fantasy would be. Her breasts were so small. He wanted to feel them in the palm of his hands. He wanted very much to touch her as she'd touched herself.

But she'd captivated him with her fantasy even before that. The whole concept of seducing a priest, with all its illicit overtones of forbidden lust and sin, held a certain appeal. He'd never done any sexual role playing before, but he had to admit that the fact she thought he was a priest and she'd once entertained fantasies about making love to one added an extra element of excitement.

And this one afternoon of forbidden pleasure was all

they would ever have. It had occurred to him while she was giving him her confession that *seize the day* had never seemed more real to him.

Once she discovered the truth about him...

Dane pushed the thought away. If one afternoon was all they would ever have, then he wanted to make the most of it for both their sakes. The piper could be paid later.

She'd won her battle with the shorts, but as they slid down her legs, Dane's gaze remained riveted to the swatch of red lace that remained. He hadn't thought it was possible for him to grow any harder, but he'd been wrong. He found himself in the same precarious position he'd been in that morning when he'd been afraid to make any quick move in the coffee shop.

And then he'd only had to deal with what it *might* be like to see her naked. Now she was here. In the flesh. When she hooked her thumbs into the thin red strips that crossed her hips, Dane took a risk by rising and moving toward her.

"You're breaking the rules," she said.

"Once you take that off, I'm going to be inside you."

"Oh." Her pulse pounded at the hollow of her throat, but her hands stilled. "If that's the direction your thoughts are headed, you're wearing too many clothes."

Keeping his eyes on hers, Dane first took off the Roman collar, then rid himself of the T-shirt and shorts.

Her eyes had become riveted to his black briefs. Her hands were at his waistband before he grabbed her wrists.

But before he trusted himself to move again, he asked

the question that needed to be asked. "Speaking of being inside of you, are you protected?"

"I'm on the pill, and I have condoms in the pocket of my shorts."

"Good to know." He had some, too, but it would be better if he didn't have to explain why a priest might be Boy Scout prepared.

Then she met his eyes. "Since my fantasy is over, I'm going to take these panties off now. Then I'm going to take off yours."

"Don't you want to hear about my fantasy?"

She blinked. "You had a fantasy?"

"Several. All about you." He was pretty sure they wouldn't be his last. He scooped up the shorts, then took her hand and led her over to the boulder he'd been sitting on. "I was in the coffee shop across the street when you selected those items of lingerie out of the display window at Discoveries. Imagining you trying them on fueled my fantasies for quite a while. I'll show you."

Over time, the boulder had been worn glassy smooth by wind and water. He lifted her up on the rock ledge and then stepped up behind her.

"I imagined joining you in that dressing room." Turning her so that she was facing the rock, he took her hands and pressed them against the smooth surface. "Keep them there." Then gripping her hips, he eased her back a foot so that she was leaning forward against the boulder.

"I'm going to touch you now."

The tremor that ran through her had his hand trembling as he trailed his fingers from her nape down the length of her spine. He paused just where the strap of the red lace thong intruded. "I've wanted to do this ever since you came out of the hotel wearing that halter top."

Her breath hitched. "What about your fantasy about the two of us in the dressing room?"

"I'll get to that." At least he hoped he would. But the way he'd positioned her against the boulder had another tempting fantasy springing into his mind.

Because he couldn't help himself, he ran his fingers down her spine again, but this time when he reached the waistband of her thong, he continued on to trace the crease of her buttocks, then slide his fingers between her legs. He stopped only when he reached the entrance to her wet heat.

Her breath hitched and another tremor ran through her. "Please." She pushed against his fingers until the tip of one of them slipped into her.

"Shhhh." He caught the lobe of her ear between his teeth and clamped down on his control. It would be so easy to put on the condom, push aside that thong and bury himself inside of her. But he'd heard the note of surprise in her voice when he'd admitted to fantasizing about her. And there was more he wanted to show her. He withdrew his hand.

When she whimpered, he said, "Soon. First, I want you to just feel."

Feel? What choice did she have? Her whole body was throbbing with sensations. The image he'd planted in her mind of him standing in that dressing room with her was so erotic. If he hadn't slipped his hands around her to cup her breasts, she wouldn't have been able to remain standing.

"Look down and watch me touch you, Naomi."

She hadn't believed she could get any hotter, but the sight of those large hands rubbing against her nipples and then moving lower and lower down her torso had her wondering why she didn't just evaporate into steam and blow away.

When he reached the red lace of the thong, he stopped.

Disappointment flooded her. "You said you were going to touch me."

"Oh, I intend to." But one hand remained where it was while the other disappeared from her sight. She watched the fingers of the hand she could still see slip beneath the red lace and into her fold to capture her clitoris. Just as quickly the fingers of his other hand were pushing into her heat.

She shot straight to the brink of a climax. For a moment, he held her there, not moving, not allowing her to move.

Then using both hands at once, he said, "Come for me, Naomi."

She cried out as the climax swept through her with the violence of a riptide, first dragging her over and under in wave after wave of pleasure, then tossing her up and over an airless peak.

10

WHEN SHE COULD THINK AGAIN, she discovered that she was straddling his lap, her head resting on his shoulder. He sat in the sand, leaning against the rock ledge they'd both stood on moments ago. Or had it been longer? Their breathing had evened. And she could feel that their heartbeats had slowed.

The waves lapping the shore were closer, and the shadow of the boulder stretched farther across the sand.

There was a part of her that didn't want to move. She liked the feel of his arm around her. Another part of her knew that their time together was slipping away, and she didn't want to waste a second.

Raising her head, she looked into his eyes. What she saw there had her blood heating and her body pulsing all over again. The hardness of his erection pressed against her leg.

"You weren't always a priest."

"No. I wasn't even a good candidate."

She recalled her initial surprise when he'd agreed so easily to her proposition—and her suspicion from the first that she was dealing with two men. "Why weren't you a good candidate?"

"I ran away from the first few foster homes I was placed in and I spent some time on the streets. I might have ended up in jail if a cop and his wife hadn't taken me in."

"You were raised by a cop?"

"An Irish Catholic one. After he'd arrested me twice, he took the time to find out about my family. Then he made me a proposition. If I followed the rules, I could live with him and his wife, and he'd help me find my brothers and sister."

"You accepted."

"I wasn't getting anywhere on my own. As it turned out, he was never able to locate them. But he never gave up."

"And you eventually became a priest and not a cop."

"His wife, Nell, encouraged me. She thought having one cop in the family was enough."

Lowering her head, she began to nibble along his neck where the collar had been and felt a quiver of response move through him.

"Naomi…"

"I haven't had enough of you yet." She framed his face with her hands. "We've both lived out our fantasies, right?"

"In a manner of speaking."

"Mine was better than yours."

He brushed her lips with his. "Not possible."

She smiled slowly. "My proposition was for one time, but I haven't made you come yet."

His erection pulsed against her.

"I think we ought to take a little break from the

fantasies and improvise," she suggested. "And I want you to be inside of me when you come. I don't want to imagine it first. I just want to do it."

"Deal."

"Get out of your briefs." She scrambled off him to grab her shorts and fish out a condom. After tearing it open with her teeth, she glanced back at him.

And stopped breathing.

He was naked and the size of his erection had her throat going dry as dust. "Much better than in my fantasy."

"I could return the compliment."

"Later," she murmured as, condom in hand, she crawled back to straddle him again. But instead of sheathing him, she clasped her fingers around his penis and then lowered her mouth to run her tongue along the length of it.

On a low moan, he thrust up hard into her hand. Then he reached for her head and threaded his fingers into her hair.

"I never imagined doing this." Starting at the base, she licked her way slowly up the length of him. "I like it."

When she closed her mouth over him and sucked, he jerked up and hissed. Encouraged, she took in more of him and sucked harder.

"Stop." The word came out on a thread of sound.

Reluctantly, she released him and met his eyes. "You don't like it."

"I love it." But when she tried to lower her head, his fingers tightened in her hair.

"Why should I stop?"

"You wanted me inside of you this time."

She smiled. "And if I want to continue improvising?"

"Two can play that game." Lifting her hips, he brought her close enough to his mouth to trace the triangle of lace covering her with his tongue. As he licked his way down one side and then the other, fire, hotter than anything she'd ever experienced before, arrowed through her. Grabbing his shoulders for support, she got her feet under her and, still squatting, arched backward to give him more access.

"Hold on. We need to get rid of these." His teeth scraped her skin as he used them to free her from the thong. "Much better."

She was vaguely aware that he twitched the condom out of her fingers and sheathed himself, but her focus was centered on the heat of his breath feathering over her clitoris.

She cried out when he tasted her with two quick flicks of his tongue. Screamed when his tongue pierced her.

She was already hovering on the brink of that final eruption of pleasure when he guided her down so that she could take him in. He controlled the entry, lowering her slowly and drawing out the pleasure for both of them. Then suddenly, as if he'd reached his breaking point, he gripped her hips and thrust into her all the way.

"Make me come, Naomi."

Once again she had no choice. She had to move, sliding up and then down. Up and then down. Cupping the nape of her neck, he drew her mouth to his, whispered, "Make me come now."

Then he kissed her, using the same slow strokes with his tongue that she was using on him. Naomi felt as if she were drowning in him—his taste, his scent, the exquisite pressure in the way he filled her. She didn't want this to end. But gradually, she couldn't help herself. The pleasure was so intense, so consuming, that she had to pick up the pace.

His tongue matched her rhythm, urging her on until her release was just there, beckoning her. Unable to help herself, she moved faster and faster until her orgasm began. Then she rode it out, rode him until she finally pulled him with her over that same peak he'd taken her to before.

IT WAS NEARLY SIX WHEN DANE let himself into his room at Haworth House. His mind was still full of Naomi and the time they'd spent together. They'd made love two more times before they'd left the secluded beach. And each time she'd taken him further than any woman had before.

Now he had to think—to get back his perspective. During those three hours on the beach he'd totally lost it. Hell, he'd lost parts of himself. He'd joined her in her fantasy and allowed himself to be Father Dane MacFarland.

He would have kept her on the beach longer—he'd have her there right now—if the tide hadn't come in. They'd had to walk through ankle-deep water to get to the path they'd followed on their climb down.

She hadn't spoken on the drive back. He hadn't, either. Because he still hadn't decided what his next move would be. And he desperately needed to figure that out.

Any idea he'd had that making love to her once or

twice or even four times was going to get her out of his system was right up there with pigs flying.

Pacing across the room, he ran a hand through his hair. He'd never been that intimate with a woman. On both physical and emotional levels, she pushed buttons that no one else ever had. Aside from the pretense that he was a priest, everything he'd told her about his life was the truth. He hadn't thought of some of it in years.

The Irish cop he'd told her about—Patrick McNally—*had* literally taken him off the streets. Patrick and his wife, Nell, had been older and childless. Although Nell had entertained dreams of him entering the seminary, they hadn't turned him into a priest or a cop. But Dane wondered if he'd be as good as he was at his job if it hadn't been for Patrick's training. The couple had died when he was eighteen, and the money they'd left him had paid for college and helped a great deal when he'd opened his business.

He'd told Ian about Patrick and Nell, of course, but no one else. Ever.

But he hadn't been able to prevent himself from telling Naomi. He stopped in front of the balcony doors and slid them open. He spotted her immediately, sitting at a table in the courtyard talking with Leo King and another man he recognized as Thomas Fairchild, a younger partner at Naomi's old firm. The two men had been waiting in the lobby with Avery when they'd returned.

The vultures who wanted the money Michael Davenport had taken from them were circling. And he wasn't the only one who suspected that Naomi held the key to that money. While they'd been having their forbidden tryst on the beach, the FBI had probably checked in to the hotel also.

For a moment, he let his mind drift back to their arrival at Haworth House. After handing over the Corvette's keys to the young man in front of the hotel, she'd turned to him and offered him her hand.

The formal gesture and the speech she delivered weren't merely a show for the hotel staff. It was a message to him that she intended to keep her part of the little bargain they'd made. What had happened between them on the beach was a one-time thing just as she'd promised. She would be discreet, and he wouldn't have to worry about her making any demands on him.

But he was going to have to worry about it. They both were. Any idea to the contrary had been banished into oblivion by the simple press of her palm against his. For one instant as desire exploded inside of him, he'd come close to tossing her into the car and just driving off with her. Consequences be damned.

But the consequences had to be faced. So did the facts. The danger he was sure she was in hadn't vanished during their little hiatus on the beach. He might have put it out of his mind for a few hours, but Davenport was somewhere on the island. And he wasn't stupid. He'd make a move very soon to take back what he'd given her, and once he had it, Naomi was disposable.

After her dismissive handshake in front of the hotel, Dane had kept his distance in the lobby, but he'd lingered long enough to hear Leo King invite her for a drink in the courtyard.

She hadn't liked the fact that King was there. He'd seen the tension return to her body, and he'd had to clamp down hard on the urge to go to her. Because he knew some of what she was feeling. Reality had just descended with a vengeance. And it was high time he focused on it.

Two days ago, Leo King had fired Naomi because of her association with Michael Davenport. So she had to be wondering what were he and his partner doing here on the Island.

And then there were the mementos that Davenport had given her. Dane had to find out more about them. Naomi didn't need a lover right now. She needed a bodyguard with a clear head and a good eye.

Swinging away from the balcony, he was halfway to the nightstand near his bed when he realized he still had the latter—a good eye—if not the former. The painting over his bed of the Belle Island lighthouse was slightly ajar. He stopped short and scanned the room. If she hadn't been filling his mind, he would have seen it sooner.

Since he'd left, someone had been in his room, and they'd searched it. Definitely not the maid. She'd been in and out, replacing towels and changing the linens, while he'd been in town.

No, someone had come into this room while he was on that beach with Naomi. He meticulously swept his gaze around the room again. The signs were subtle, but he had a trained eye. The zipper on his suitcase was fully closed. He'd left it partially open. The duffel he'd taken into town was closer to the center of his bed than the edge. Striding to his closet, he saw that the door was closed tightly. He'd left it ajar. Inside, he saw that the hangers had been shifted.

He'd definitely become a person of interest to someone. Moving back to the bed, he ran his hand along the edges of the lighthouse painting and located the bug on the side closest to the phone. Leaving it there, Dane decided to postpone his phone call to Ian until he could find a more private venue.

By the time he stepped out onto his balcony, his mind was clearer than it had been all day. And he wasn't thinking of fantasies. He was planning how he was going to get into Naomi's room and find out if it had been bugged, too.

She was still sitting at table talking to her former bosses. He glanced over at her room. This was as good a time as any to pay a quick visit. Then he caught the flicker of movement in the tower windows above her balcony. Whirling, he strode to his duffel and grabbed the tools he would need.

Someone was in that tower room right now.

NAOMI HAD JUST TAKEN HER SEAT and was still trying to gather her thoughts when Tess set a glass of white wine down in front of her. "Is there anything else I can get for you?"

Naomi smiled at Tess. "No, this is fine."

"I asked her to open a bottle of Pouilly-Fuissé and to bring you a glass the moment you arrived," Leo said.

"Thank you." It was Leo who had introduced her to the French burgundy, but as Naomi lifted the glass to take a polite sip, she thought she would have preferred a brandy. Her mind was still so full of Dane, and she really had to shift her focus.

Back to reality. Finding Leo King and Thomas Fairchild in the lobby waiting for her had helped a great deal. Not even a new wardrobe and mind-blowing sex on the beach were going to free her from the old Naomi's past.

"Aren't you going to ask us why we're here?" Thomas asked.

Naomi looked at him. Leo may have been a father figure to her, but she'd never thought of Thomas as a brother. Though he'd been practicing law for several years when she'd joined the firm, she'd always sensed that he'd felt threatened by her. And she recalled the smug and satisfied look on his face the morning that Leo told her the firm could no longer afford to have her associated with them. "Why are you here?"

"Thomas and I think we may have been hasty in letting you go," Leo explained. "Thomas, why don't you tell her the good news."

Thomas cleared his throat. "Leo and I would like you to come back to your job."

Surprised, she looked from one man to the other. "Why?"

Thomas glanced at Leo.

"Go ahead, Thomas," Leo said. "Tell her."

"We don't think we gave you the support and loyalty you deserve."

Naomi directed her words to Leo. "Nothing has changed. I was engaged to Michael Davenport. Through me he gained access to the two of you and many of our top clients. If I come back to the firm, I'll be a constant reminder of that."

"Be that as it may," Leo said, "we think we may have damaged the reputation of the firm even more by letting you go. Dismissing you makes it look as though we believe you were involved in some way in the swindle. And that fuels the rumors that perhaps we were involved also."

Naomi's brows shot up. "Clients believe that you were involved?"

"There have been some grumblings to that effect,"

Thomas said, the anger clear in his voice. "Ridiculous. We were taken in by that charlatan, too."

Leo laid a hand on hers. "Just as you were, my dear. Thomas and I have discussed the matter. By letting you go we fed into those suspicions. Taking you back will strengthen our position that we were all victims—just as they were."

Naomi considered the argument he was making. In an odd way, it did make sense, she supposed.

Leo released her hand. "If you could pack your things, we'd like to take the early ferry back to the mainland tomorrow. The Middleton case goes to trial day after tomorrow, and I'd like you to take second chair. I know how hard you worked on the research. Winning it should be a slam dunk."

Naomi studied the two men for a moment. Thomas's smile might not have reached his eyes, but it was there. Leo was literally beaming. She could have her job back.

And they had no doubt at all that she would accept their offer. Evidently, they considered her a slam dunk also. Anger flickered to life inside of her. The Naomi who'd ridden over to the island on the ferry yesterday wouldn't have had to think twice. But…

She knew the moment that Dane stepped out on his balcony. Every nerve in her body snapped to attention. Her blood quickened and she could feel the heat of his gaze on her back. Very deliberately she reached for her wineglass, hoping the coolness of the liquid would quench the fire that had flared to life inside of her again.

For a moment, she felt trapped between the man behind her and the two men in front of her. Then suddenly, she knew that Dane was gone.

Leo touched his glass to the one she'd raised. "A toast. To the future of King and Fairchild. May it one day be King, Fairchild and Brightman."

"No." Naomi set her glass down on the table without sipping any of the wine.

"No?" Leo asked. "What are you saying?"

"I'll have to think about your offer, Leo. But I certainly won't be leaving on the ferry tomorrow morning. I still have a few loose ends to tie up here. In the meantime, I hope you enjoy your stay at Haworth House."

Rising, she walked back into the lobby and very nearly plowed into Sheriff Nate Kirby. He grabbed her by the shoulders to steady her.

"Naomi, wait."

She turned to see that Leo and Thomas had followed her, but they stopped when they saw the sheriff.

"Is there a problem, Officer?" Leo asked.

"I just have a few questions for Ms. Brightman."

"She'll need an attorney present," Leo said.

"Leo, if I need an attorney, I'll represent myself. And you have the only answer you're going to get for now." She summoned up a smile. "But I do want you to enjoy your stay. Dinner's on the house."

Leo King didn't like it, but he turned and let Thomas follow him back into the courtyard.

"Who is that?" Nate asked as he led the way to a cluster of chairs that weren't occupied.

"My former boss. He came all the way out here to offer me my job back."

Nate gestured her into a chair and then sat across from her. "He must really want you."

She frowned. "Yes." Then she met his eyes. "Do you have news about that license plate?"

"Not yet. I received a call from the FBI Boston

bureau. They were checking to see if you were by any chance here on Belle Island. Until the local police called the bureau, the men they had watching you were still under the impression that you were in your apartment."

She lifted her chin. "No one told me I had to stay in Boston."

Nate's lips curved. "Did you tell your ex-boss where you were going?"

"No." Frowning again, she glanced back at the courtyard. "But once anyone discovered I wasn't in Boston, this would be the obvious place to look."

"The FBI is not happy that you didn't tell them your travel plans, but they had some information that I thought you should know."

"What?"

"The reason the local police discovered you weren't in your apartment is they received a call from one of your neighbors reporting that your apartment had been broken into and ransacked."

Fear knotted in her belly. "When?"

"The neighbor wasn't sure. Could have been either yesterday or earlier today. She discovered it when she got home from work this afternoon and let herself in to water your plants."

Naomi's mind began to race. "Who?"

Nate studied her. "Wild guess—someone thinks you hold the key to the money that Michael Davenport swindled his clients out of. And whoever broke in figured they could find it."

DANE RACED UP THE SERVICE STAIRS, taking them two at a time. It had cost him precious minutes to avoid both the courtyard and the lobby, but he didn't want to attract either Naomi's or her former boss's attention. The last exit door only got him to the second level. He knew from the brief tour he'd given himself on the day he'd done his reconnaissance that the tower room was still two floors above him.

The first flight of stairs was stone, and he raced up them and down the corridor. The paneled oak door to the tower room boasted an old-fashioned lock, and he wasted a few more precious moments getting past it. Then he stepped quietly into a dark stairwell. The cold hit him immediately and set his nerves dancing.

The iron staircase rose in a circle into darkness. There was probably a light switch, but whoever was up in the tower room hadn't chosen to flip it. He slowed his pace, climbing slowly so that he didn't make any noise. And he listened. All he heard was the distant and muted sound of the sea.

The darkness gradually dissipated as he rounded the last turn in the staircase and an open archway came into view. Dust motes danced in the streams of daylight pouring in through the circle of windows. The room should have been stuffy and heated by the sunshine, but it was bone-chillingly cold. And part of the room was blocked from his view. A tingle of warning snaked up his spine.

He wasn't alone in the room.

Drawing out his gun, Dane gripped it in both hands, intending to fan the area that he hadn't yet seen.

As he stepped into the room, he caught the blur of movement to his right. He tried to swivel, but the blow to his temple sent him toppling to the floor. His gun skidded away. Basic survival instinct had him rolling, but not fast enough to avoid the second blow to his thigh.

Pain sang up his leg, but he managed to scramble to his knees. Through the stars still spinning in front of his eyes, he saw Michael Davenport swing the poker up over his head.

Dane threw up his hands but he wasn't going to be able to avoid it. Michael Davenport had a good chance of finishing the job he'd started three years ago.

Then there was another rush of cold and a flash of light behind him, and inches away from him, the poker halted in its downward arc as if it had slammed into some kind of shield. Davenport's face had gone bone white and sweat sheened his skin as he stared at a space beyond Dane's shoulders.

Dane felt along the floor beside him and located his gun, but before he could raise it, Davenport took two stumbling steps back, then screamed.

The sound filled the room muting the clatter of the poker as it fell to the floor. Then Davenport turned and ran from the room.

11

NAOMI'S HEAD WAS SPINNING as she let herself into her room. She had to think. Who had searched her apartment and what did Leo's job offer mean?

But her mind kept looping back to the scene in front of the hotel before reality had intruded. It had been so hard to shake Dane's hand and say goodbye. She'd spent most of the ride home rehearsing the little speech. But there'd been a moment when she'd first taken his hand that the words, her promise— Everything had drained away. All she was aware of was the press of his palm against hers, the heat of his eyes on her skin and the intensity of the desire that burned so fiercely inside of her.

She still wasn't sure how her legs had carried her up the steps and into the lobby. No matter what her mind said, her body might not be able to give Dane MacFarland up. It was that simple. That basic.

Of course, that was the whole problem with forbidden fruit. It tasted so good you had to experience it again.

But evidently she hadn't morphed totally into a new and reckless Naomi. She hadn't followed her instincts, pushed him back into the Corvette, and driven off with him. There was enough of the old Naomi in her to make her want to keep her word, and she'd made the terms of her proposition clear.

Big whoop!

Sinking onto the foot of her bed now, she propped her elbows on her knees and cupped her chin with her hands. The fact that Leo King and Thomas Fairchild had been waiting for her in the lobby and insisted she join them for a drink had brought her back to earth with a little jolt.

And the job offer. Why hadn't she snapped it up? Was it because of Dane?

The man had certainly gotten to her. When she'd entered the lobby, her aim had been to hurry to her room and spend a quiet evening, one in which she could relive every single moment of the time she'd spent on the beach with him.

Okay, so what if that smacked of the way she'd handled her priest-crush at fourteen? After the afternoon she'd spent with Dane, wasn't she entitled?

Rising, she paced to the balcony doors and then back to her bed. For all she cared, the new Naomi could sue the old one. Or vice versa. And the dispute could be settled out of court since she was now going to spend her evening trying to figure out why Leo King wanted her back and why someone had ransacked her apartment in Boston.

Okay, so the real world had come knocking at her door. What had she expected? Yesterday on the ferry ride over, she'd known that her retreat wouldn't remain solitary for very long. For all she knew, some FBI agents had already checked in to Haworth House, too.

Without realizing it, she'd paced back to the balcony

doors again. For one moment, she was tempted to open them and see if she could catch a glimpse of Dane.

Her hand was on the knob when she heard it—the sound of a thud overhead. Alarm shot through her as she looked up at the ceiling.

Someone was in Hattie's tower room.

She raced out to the hall and down to the carved oak door. She was still a few feet away when she saw it was ajar. Her heart jumped to her throat and fluttered like a frightened bird.

She'd locked the door when she'd left earlier, and no one but Avery on the hotel staff had a key. She reached for the knob, intending to pull it open, then froze when she heard the scream. A man's scream, followed by footsteps thundering down the stairs. The door burst open, propelling her backward and slamming her head into the wall. Stars spun in front of her eyes, but she still caught a glimpse of the man as he tore down the corridor and through the door to the stone staircase.

Shock hit first. Then as the freeze-framed moment burned itself into her brain, recognition sank in with the impact of a bare-fisted punch.

In spite of the fact he was wearing a baseball cap, she wasn't mistaken. During the past six months, she'd had plenty of opportunity to study that profile—the long, almost Roman nose, the smooth jawline. And the tattoo on his upper arm didn't fool her this time.

"Michael!" She'd intended to shout the name, but all she managed was a whisper of sound. She pushed herself away from the wall, intending to run after him.

Then she heard the moan and whirled back to the staircase. The sound had come from Hattie's tower room. Without another thought, she took the iron stairs two at a time.

She found him sitting on the floor near the archway, holding his head in one hand. A fireplace poker lay near him.

"Dane?"

He got to his feet.

"What happened? Are you all—" The sentence faded away when she saw the gun.

Moving swiftly toward her, he tucked it into the back of his waistband in a quick, competent move.

"What are you doing with a—"

He stopped her sentence by placing a hand over her mouth and urging her back against the wall.

A suspicion formed in her mind, and she tried to dismiss it. Then he leaned down and whispered in her ear, "We can't talk here. Tell me that the cut on my head needs attention, and there's a first-aid kit in the bathroom."

A cut on his head? A bubble of hysteria rose in her throat and she fought against it. When he removed his hand and stepped back, she saw the blood dripping down his cheek. He'd been hurt. For the moment, she focused her attention on that. "You're bleeding. There's a first-aid kit in the bathroom." On shaky legs, she led the way.

Once inside, he flipped on the light switch and locked the door. The room was small; a sink and a toilet lined one wall and a small stall shower filled the corner. He only had to take one step to reach the shower knobs and twist them. The sound of running water filled the space.

"Why are you doing that?" she asked. Of all the questions tumbling around in her mind, that one seemed the safest.

"Whoever was here may have bugged the room."

Michael—it had been Michael who was here. Why would he bug the room? And why would Dane— She thought of the gun again. "What were you doing here?"

"I was on my balcony and I saw someone in the tower windows."

So you raced up here with a gun? Something squeezed around her heart. In a moment, she was going to sort through it, figure out what it meant. For now, to steady herself, Naomi opened the cabinet over the sink and located bandages, antiseptic, cotton gauze. Her hand only trembled a little as she lined them up on the glass shelf.

When she closed the cabinet door, she saw his face in the mirror behind hers. With his hair mussed and blood on his cheek, he looked dangerous. Not at all like the man she'd spent the afternoon with on the beach. But hadn't she sensed two men in Dane MacFarland from the very first?

More questions pushed at the edge of her mind, but she ignored them and gestured him to sit down on the toilet seat. Then she focused her entire attention on the task. Noting the spot where the blood had begun to mat his hair, she leaned closer to examine it as she probed gently with her fingers. "It's not deep. I don't think you'll need stitches."

"Good to know." His breath hissed out as she swabbed it with antiseptic.

After pressing a clean piece of gauze over the wound, she replaced her hand with his. "Hold it there for a bit to stop the bleeding."

"You're good at this," he said.

"I had a lot of practice while my sisters and I were growing up." The fact that her voice was steady shocked her. Because her insides felt like jelly. And there was a tightness in her chest that was making it hard to breathe.

She moved to the wall where he'd been standing so that she could face him directly. They were still close. Her knees were less than a foot away from his. If he stood up, there was no way to avoid contact. In spite of her questions, in spite of what had to be the answer, the thought of touching him triggered a surge of desire she was helpless to prevent.

A tiny flame of anger flared to life inside of her, and for the first time since she'd raced up the iron stairs, her head began to clear. "You're not a priest."

"No."

Though she'd known it, hearing him speak that one word sent a little stab of pain through her. That made her more angry. "Who are you?" she demanded. "FBI?"

"No."

The one-word answers combined with his calm, even tone forced her to clamp down hard on her temper. She badly wanted to hit him. She'd give in to that temptation later. Right now she wanted answers.

"Who are you then, and why are you really here at Haworth House?"

Dane took a moment to study her. His brain was cooler now. They were in a locked bathroom, and there was little likelihood that Michael Davenport would be coming back. Something had happened out there, something he couldn't explain. Davenport had had the poker raised over his head, prepared to execute the final deadly blow. Then he'd frozen in place. Dane didn't think he'd ever forget the scream.

For now he pushed that concern aside. Figuring out how to handle the current situation required his full attention. Naomi had had a shock, but she was rallying. Her hands had stopped trembling while she'd been fussing with his head, and she was pretty easy to read. Right now she was spitting mad. He considered how much to tell her.

"Fine."

As she stepped toward the door, her leg brushed against his. The space was so confined that neither of them could move without touching the other.

"If you don't want to tell me, I'll let you explain your presence in the tower room to Sheriff Kirby. He was still in the lobby a few moments ago when I came up to my room."

Rising, he slapped a hand on the door and managed to grab her wrist before she could unlock it. Clearly, she was going to have to have it all. "What was Kirby doing here?"

She turned to face him, and they were close enough that their bodies brushed for just an instant. Dane felt the searing heat at each contact point. She felt it, too. He could see it in her eyes.

She lifted her chin. "You answer my question first, Mr. MacFarland. If that's your name."

Neither of them looked down at where his hand still gripped her wrist, but she had to be aware of how fast her pulse was racing. He certainly was. Very carefully, he released her and stepped back to sit down on the toilet seat. "My real name is Dane MacFarland."

She leaned back against the bathroom door and folded her arms across her chest. "And your *real* reason for being here?"

"I'm looking for Michael Davenport." He saw the flash of pain in her eyes and silently cursed himself.

"Who are you working for?"

"Myself. My brother Ian and I run MacFarland Investigations. But we don't have a client on this one. This is personal. Three years ago I nearly had him, but he got away."

"Tell me."

"It's a long story."

"Not as long as the one I could invent to tell Sheriff Kirby. Of course, you may check out, but explaining yourself to local law enforcement might slow you down some."

Dane nodded. "Okay. Three years ago, I was hired by a bank in Kansas City to help them locate Davenport and to get back the money he'd swindled people out of. He was using a different alias, but the scam was pretty much the same. He started there with a local candy company and got them to turn over management of the employees' retirement fund to him. In the process, he became engaged to the owner's daughter. The man had a solid reputation, and when word spread of the initial profits his company was making, other investors came knocking at Davenport's door. Then one day, he and the money vanished."

"That's exactly what happened in Boston."

"Yes. He used the same pattern. But in Boston, he got some coverage in the press. That's what drew him to my attention."

"How does he get away with it?"

"He's very good with computers. Everything looks fine on the surface. The money appears to be there. When the forensic accountants finally cut their way through the dummy corporations and fake investment reports, they discovered the money wasn't there at all. Instead, it had been deposited into various local banks and withdrawn over time in such small enough amounts that it never triggered any warning bells. The largest amount they located was two million, and it had been withdrawn just a few days before Davenport had disappeared."

"What does he do—hide it in a mattress until he decides to take off?"

"It's not that easy to transport large amounts of cash. Or to hide them. A wire transfer to some offshore bank would be the easiest way to go. But transfers can be traced. So I developed this theory."

Her brows shot up. "Don't keep me in suspense."

The dryness of her tone nearly made him smile. "I developed a theory that proved correct in Kansas City. When Davenport thinks the scam has run its course, he withdraws the money in small amounts and purchases a portable artifact of appropriate value."

"Portable?" Her brow furrowed. "Like in *Charade*, the Cary Grant/Audrey Hepburn movie where her ex-husband put all the money into a rare stamp."

"Something like that."

"It's a way to launder the money," she said in a musing tone. "Then when he's safely established in a new identity, he sells whatever pricey object he has, deposits the money and starts a new scam."

She took a step away from the door as if she wanted to pace. Then she stopped and met his eyes. "You said you nearly had him in Kansas City."

"He was working with a partner, a woman. She helped him make his initial contacts, vouched for him. But she'd begun to mistrust him. Smart lady. Michael Davenport doesn't play well with others. She managed to get hold of the artifact, a bronze figurine, and she was holding it until Davenport turned over her share of the cash. I approached her, and once she knew someone was on to her, it was fairly easy to convince her to help me set a trap."

"What happened?"

"I was with her when he came to get it. We were standing as close as you and I are standing right now. He got in without my hearing him. He shot both of us. I survived. She didn't."

Naomi's hand flew to her throat. She wanted to say that Michael wouldn't do that. But the man who'd run down the corridor, the man who'd hit Dane, wasn't the man she'd known as Michael Davenport. He was a stranger.

And so was the man sitting on the toilet seat, she reminded herself. The pain settled in her stomach this time, a dull throbbing ache. She really didn't know him at all. "You think I'm Michael's partner."

"No."

She saw the anger flash in his eyes and it did something to ease the pain.

"The FBI might have thought so at first, but they're beginning to have their doubts. I think he used you to get access to King and Fairchild and their clients. Then when the curtain came down faster than he'd expected on his scam, I think he stashed the artifact with you until he could pick it up."

"So that's why you came here and got close to me, made love to me?"

Fury radiated from him as he rose off the seat and stepped toward her. She felt a flutter of panic and excitement as she backed in to the door.

"No. I came here to catch a thief and a murderer. Do you think I planned on wanting you from the first moment I saw you? Masquerading as a priest was supposed to put up an insurmountable barrier between us.

I intended to gain your trust without making you think that I had any sexual intentions. Instead, that's all I've had since I laid eyes on you. You weren't supposed to get inside of me until I can't think of anyone or anything but you. What happened between us should never have happened."

She might have needed the door for support, but she kept her eyes steady on his. "But it did happen."

"Yes."

And they were both remembering exactly what had happened between them. He wasn't touching her, but he was so close she could feel the heat of him in every pore. And she recalled exactly what his hands had felt like on her skin. The room, already tiny, grew even smaller. He still smelled of the sea, and with each breath she took, the memories of what had happened on the beach grew more intense.

His breath feathered over her cheek and all she could think of was how much she wanted his mouth on hers again. She had to experience again the mindless whirl of pleasure that only he could bring her. She simply had to. She was rising on her toes to close the distance when she caught herself.

She couldn't. In denial, in desperation, she placed two hands on his chest and gave him a hard shove. But the moment she felt the thunder of his heartbeat, her fingers curled into his shirt and she dragged him closer.

"This is crazy." But she couldn't stop her body from melting against his when she was finally pressed against him. "We're crazy."

"Yeah." But his mouth was already doing things to the curve of her throat. "We'll go into therapy tomorrow."

She nearly cried out in protest when he drew back

enough to grip her arms and draw her up until they were eye-to-eye. "No fantasy this time, Naomi."

"No fantasy," she agreed as a dark thrill moved through her.

"This time it's just you and me."

And that was exactly the way she wanted it. Whoever he was. "Kiss me. I can't wait another minute."

"Say my name."

"Dane."

When his mouth finally crushed hers, there was none of the gentleness, none of the careful exploration that she'd experienced before. She didn't want it. She wanted this. With each nip and scrape of his teeth, the torrid heat that only he could trigger battered her again and again.

She'd sampled his flavors, savored them, but the desperation was new. At the first taste of it, her own response overwhelmed her. She was dimly aware of the hiss of the shower and the moist heat filling the room, but all she really knew were his lips and his hands. As eager as he was, she helped him pull off her shirt and drag down her shorts.

Then at last his hands were on her, searching—not with the gentleness he'd shown earlier, but with a bruising meticulousness. Those hard fingers, those rough palms, scraped her skin from breast to hips, stoking old fires, kindling fresh ones.

How could he possibly make her want more, feel more than she had just a few hours ago?

"More," she said on a ragged breath. "Now."

Her desperate murmur sent Dane teetering toward the thin edge of sanity. And he should have been more prepared. This wasn't the first time. He'd kissed her before. He'd touched her before. He should have known what to expect. But from the moment he tasted her, desire escalated to the raw and the primitive. There seemed to be no way to prepare for explosions of need that she could set off inside of him. No way to control his response.

Pushing her back against the bathroom door, he let his hands feast on her—soft skin, strong muscle. But it wasn't enough. He needed more. Helpless, driven to possess, he plunged two fingers into her and sent her shooting over the edge.

It was his name she cried out, and it still wasn't enough. Lifting her hips, he set her on the narrow counter. His blood was pounding in his head, screaming in his loins for release. It seemed he'd waited all his life and not a mere matter of hours to have her again.

His breath was ragged, his eyes fused on hers as he released himself and put on the condom. He dug his fingers into her hips again, drawing her forward to the edge of the counter, and positioned himself between her legs. Then he plunged into her, hard and deep. She closed around him, a tight, hot glove.

She dug her nails into his shoulders and wrapped her legs around him. "This time come with me."

He pulled out and drove into her again and again. When the next convulsion rippled through her, her muscles clamped around him, owned him, and dragged him with her over the edge.

12

NAOMI WIPED THE REMAINING FOG off the bathroom mirror and took a long, hard look at herself. She wished that she could clear the fog out of her brain just as easily.

The shower had helped, but the woman she saw in the mirror, her hair slicked back, her body wrapped in a white towel, still looked like she'd been ravished. Her lips were swollen, her skin was flushed, and unless her imagination was working overtime, her eyes held knowledge that they'd never had before.

All thanks to Dane MacFarland. A man who'd lied to her. But her body wanted him anyway, anytime, anyhow. She frowned at herself. There were other considerations, ones that required her brain to function.

Which clearly wasn't something that she could depend on when Dane MacFarland was around.

He seemed to be a little more in control. And she wasn't sure how she felt about that. Annoyed? Hurt? Jealous? What she knew for certain was that after their bout of fast, hot, mindless sex, he'd recovered enough to tell her to lock the bathroom door while he got her fresh clothes and looked for "bugs."

"Bugs." She was still trying to get her mind around the idea that Michael Davenport was bugging her room, Hattie's room and Lord knew what else? And twice now he'd hurt Dane.

She thought of the scream she'd heard just before he'd flown out of the stairwell and sent her crashing into the wall. It had been the scream of a frightened man. How was it that in the six months she'd been engaged to Michael, she'd never seen anything but the suave, smooth and seemingly caring man?

There'd been both violence and fear in the man who'd burst out of Hattie's room and raced down the hall as if the hound of the Baskervilles was on his tail.

At least her eyes were now open to the true Michael Davenport. She should be grateful for that.

And she hadn't been quite as stupid about Dane. Hadn't she sensed from the beginning that there was something very unpriestlike about him?

When the knock sounded at the door, she jumped and nearly screamed. Dane hadn't been gone more than three or four minutes.

"It's Dane. I've brought some clothes."

She flipped the lock and took the clothes he passed through a crack in the door. When he quickly closed it in her face, it was relief and not disappointment she felt. He was being practical. She sent herself a quelling look in the mirror. Practical. Didn't that used to be her middle name?

There was a dangerous man somewhere in the hotel who'd planted listening devices, killed his former partner and tried to kill Dane twice. It was time to turn back into the old Naomi and not the time to fantasize about being ravished again.

WHILE NAOMI WAS DRESSING, Dane checked the tower room. There was no trace of the almost crippling cold he'd sensed when he'd first climbed the stairs. And he hadn't felt it when he'd left the bathroom earlier.

He located a listening device on the back of the computer and left it there. He'd left the one he'd found in Naomi's bedroom similarly undisturbed. But the tower room was larger. Turning, Dane took a moment to study the space. There was a six-foot-tall partition that bisected most of the round room. That was what had blocked his view and allowed Davenport to get the jump on him.

One side of the room was furnished as a work space, and the other side had antique furniture arranged in a comfortable sitting area. Bookshelves framed a fireplace on an inner wall, and next to them were the sliding glass doors to a balcony. He searched the room quickly, locating another listening device in a vase of artificial flowers, and finally he stepped out onto the balcony. It was wide, bordered with a wrought-iron railing and protected by an awning. A table, chairs and two lounges filled the space nicely. The bug was beneath the edge of the table. This one he removed and placed back in the tower room before returning to the balcony.

The question that had been plaguing him since he'd left the bathroom was where could he take Naomi to talk. Their rooms were out and so was the tower room. Since he couldn't trust himself to keep his hands off her, bathrooms and beaches were out. What they needed was a semipublic place where they could talk without fear of being interrupted or overheard.

The balcony wasn't ideal, but this one offered more privacy because it didn't look out over the courtyard. Instead, it provided a view of the terraced gardens that led up to the cliff edge on this side of the hotel. Twilight had settled, lights twinkled in the gazeboes, and lanterns glowed along steps that led from one terrace to another. To his right, he could just make out the hedge that bordered the huge maze.

The garden wasn't an ideal location, either, but when Naomi joined him on the balcony, the look in her eyes told him that she was going to have to have answers soon.

Without saying a word, he gestured her into one of the chairs and closed the balcony doors.

"How's your head?" she asked.

"It aches."

"Would you like some brandy? Jillian keeps the wet bar well-stocked."

"I'll pass." He sat down in the chair across from her. She wore the T-shirt and shorts he'd grabbed from her room, and with her hair pulled back into a slick ponytail, she looked like a teenager. And she still stirred his blood.

Naomi folded her hands on the table. "Look, I have questions. Tons of them. I'm sure you do, too. But I want to settle something first."

"Okay."

"We have to get a handle on what's happening between us."

Though he agreed, he said, "What's happening between us?"

She broke her hands apart to wave one of them. "Lust."

He couldn't have said why the word annoyed him. She was right on the money. *Lust* was a very accurate word for what had overpowered him in the bathroom. Primitive. Raw. Nearly as basic as the need to survive. He'd never wanted a woman more, and he'd never taken one with less thought or finesse.

He should have let it go, let her go on talking. Instead, he leaned forward. "I'm not sure that lust covers everything that went on at the beach this afternoon."

She met his gaze squarely. "That was different. That was fantasy. And it's over. I'm not sure what happened in the bathroom is over."

"Okay." She'd hit the nail on the head there. "So what's your point?"

"The point is, neither one of us likes what's going on between us. So that ought to give us an edge in making sure that it doesn't happen again."

"I can guarantee that we'll make love again."

Naomi placed both palms flat on the table and rose from her chair. "Not until we have Michael Davenport in custody. Catching him has to be our first priority."

"I agree we have to get our priorities straight. I'm just not making any promises." Not ones he wasn't sure he could keep.

Naomi swallowed hard as she firmly ignored the thrill Dane's words sent rippling through her. Lord help her, she didn't want any promises. She wanted him— and he was purposely baiting her. She took a deep breath and counted to ten. It was a technique she'd often used when dealing with her sisters. Then she tried a new tack. "Look, we're both adults."

"I'll definitely agree to that."

His grin was quick and charming, and for a second she lost track of her train of thought. Fighting to get it back, she said, "Can we at least agree to do our best to keep our lust in check? That man has tried to kill you twice. I think catching him deserves our full attention."

Rising, he raised his hands, palms outward. "You're right." Then in a move so quick she couldn't avoid it, he gripped her chin in his hand and gave her a quick kiss on the nose. "Teasing you is almost as irresistible as making love to you. But I agree we should do our best to put what we're feeling on the back burner until we get Davenport."

She studied him for a moment, not quite sure if she'd gotten him on the same page she was on. He was a complicated man. Not the priest she'd first thought him to be, and more than the focused investigator he claimed to be. But thinking about Dane in any way was a distraction she couldn't afford.

Ruthlessly, she shifted her focus back to Michael. "While I was getting dressed, I thought about your idea. You think when Michael got wind of the fact that the curtain was about to crash down on his scam, he gave me a very expensive artifact to hold on to. Why? Why didn't he just cut his losses, take the money and run?"

"Lots of reasons. For one because he's greedy. He doesn't like to leave a job until the last dollar has been squeezed out. So it could have been that he was waiting for a big influx of cash from a client. Plus, I think he's a risk junkie. He loves the thrill of skating on thin ice and waiting until his pursuers are close before he figuratively thumbs his nose at them and does his little vanishing act. Or there might have been a more practical reason. Maybe there was just a delay in getting the cash converted into an artifact."

With a frown, Naomi nodded. "Besides, he had a convenient patsy to deposit the artifact with and then lie low until the coast was clear. He knew me, so he'd have a pretty good idea that I'd eventually come here to Belle Island, where it would be a lot less risky to make contact with me."

She met his eyes. "I'm figuring the artifact is one of those little gifts he gave me. Or it's hidden in one of them."

"That would be my guess."

Naomi's frown deepened. "Except he had to be sure that I would bring them with me. I kept them on a shelf in my apartment. Every time he came over, he'd inspect them. I could tell that he was pleased that I valued them. And I—just like a stupid little patsy—brought them with me. Because I was clinging to the hope that some of what he'd told me was real."

She whirled, paced to the balcony railing, and then turned back. "I absolutely hate the fact that he could be so sure I would bring those stupid things with me. I despise that I was so gullible."

He moved to her then. "You weren't."

"I certainly was."

Taking her hands, he simply held them. "No. You weren't completely taken in by everything he was telling you. If you had been, you wouldn't have settled for his let's-take-it-slowly-because-you're-such-a good-little-Catholic-girl routine. And you'd have had him in your bed."

She stared at him as the words sunk in. How could he possibly understand her better than she understood herself?

"And maybe there's a simpler explanation. Perhaps he didn't expect you to bring all of them with you. Just one."

She continued to stare at him. "Of course. The one that he could depend on me to take was the key chain he gave me from the gift shop at the Four Seasons. He even made a point of fastening all my keys to it." Withdrawing her hands from his, she fisted them on her hips and tapped her foot.

"That answers one of my questions," Dane said.

"Which one?" Naomi said, trying to control the anger she was feeling. "Just how big a sap is Naomi Brightman?"

"No. You're not a sap. Michael Davenport is a clever man who reads people very well. He's made a living lying to people and using them. So don't waste your anger on yourself. Save it for him—when we catch him."

She studied him for a moment. "You're right. What question *did* you get an answer to?"

"Why he hired someone to snatch your purse this morning."

"And hiring someone...that raises another question. Why *did* he hire those two men especially if he's a risk junkie? He was in town this morning."

"You saw him, too?"

Her eyes narrowed. "I think so. There was a man on the patio of that restaurant by the pier. He made a gesture that caught my eye, but I was thrown off by the tattoo."

She patted her upper arm. "I'd never seen Michael with one. But the man who screamed and raced out of here was definitely Michael and there was a tattoo on his upper right arm."

Dane nodded. "He was definitely on that patio near the pier this morning. He lost his hat leaning over the railing while he was trying to see if that goon managed to get your purse."

"So why did he bother to hire someone?"

Leaning his hip against the railing, Dane studied her for a moment. "That's an excellent question and deserves another. What if he didn't hire them?"

Excitement leapt to her eyes. "Then someone else did. Someone who knows about the artifact and just where it might be located. That means there's more than one person who's after it."

And that puts you in even more danger, Dane thought.

"Maybe it's the same person who ransacked my apartment early this morning," Naomi said.

He straightened and gripped her upper arms. "Someone searched your apartment back in Boston?"

"That's what Sheriff Kirby told me before I left the lobby. He came all the way out to the hotel to tell me in person. It couldn't have been Michael. He was here on the island. Besides, Michael knew that I would bring the key chain with me. After all, I'd have to lock up my apartment when I left."

A sudden crash from below had him pulling her into his arms and down behind the protection of the stone railing.

"What?" Her voice was muffled because he'd flattened her tightly against him.

"Knee-jerk reaction. The more people who know you have a key chain worth millions, the more danger that puts you in."

A curse floated up from below.

"Here, let me help," a female voice said. Then there was only the sound of cutlery striking against plates.

One of the waitstaff had obviously dropped a tray. Dane should have let her go then and helped her to her feet. But for a moment, he didn't. He couldn't. And it had nothing to do with protecting her.

Odd. He felt nothing of the heat that he'd experienced every time they'd come in contact before. Just a slowly spreading warmth. Seconds ticked by. He had no idea how many. All he knew was that he could have gone on holding Naomi Brightman just like this for a very long time.

It was Naomi who finally spoke. "I should show you the key chain."

"Right." Their faces were close enough that he could feel her breath on his skin. But before he let her up, he said, "This is more than lust, Naomi."

He watched both uncertainty and panic flash in her eyes. Fair enough, he thought. He was feeling a mix of those very same things. He drew her to her feet. "We can't talk once we go back in the tower room. Davenport planted two listening devices and I added the one I found out here. Plus, we'll need a safe room to talk once you retrieve the key chain. I've left all the bugs he planted in place just in case we can use them to our advantage."

"Got it covered," Naomi said before she led the way back into the tower. "Follow me."

IN THE SHADOWS AFFORDED by a tall hedge, Michael Davenport watched Naomi and the man masquerading as a priest disappear into the tower room. Time was running out on him, and he wanted his money. Both she and the gun-toting fake priest would pay for making him wait like this.

And for what had happened in the tower room.

Just thinking about it had his heart rate picking up.

In the confines of the maze, he'd paced off the icy fear that had paralyzed him for those few terrifying seconds in that room. And he'd finally figured it out. His mind had been temporarily affected by the damn cold and the fact that the money hadn't been where he'd expected to find it—easily accessible in her rooms.

Anger had taken hold, and for a moment all he'd known was a blind fury that Naomi hadn't played her part the way she was supposed to. Even then, he might have gotten himself under control if the fake priest hadn't come up the stairs.

The only thing he clearly recalled after that was that he'd picked up the fireplace poker and hit the priest. He remembered the sound, the sight of the man falling. But everything else was all disjointed images. Some were auditory—the scream, footsteps pounding down the iron staircase. Others were visual. There'd been a flash of light that had temporarily blinded him. Then he could picture himself running down the stairwell, through the back exit door and finally into the shelter of the maze.

But he had the anger controlled now. And it was Naomi who'd made the mistake. He knew her better than she knew herself. For that reason he was sure she'd brought the money to the island. He just had to figure out where she'd put it.

And there was only one person who could tell him. Once she did, she would pay. And so would the man helping her.

13

DANE FOLLOWED NAOMI INTO a room no larger than a closet. Five feet by seven, he estimated. Very tight quarters once the door slid shut behind them. He had to duck his head slightly to avoid the one bare light-bulb overhead. He spotted Naomi's tote right inside the door, and when he squatted down to pick it up, his head smacked hard into hers.

"Ouch." They both spoke at once.

He grabbed her shoulders to steady her. "You all right?"

"Fine. You're the one who got rapped in the head with a poker."

"I'm good." He released her shoulders and began to squat down again.

This time their knees bumped and they grabbed hands.

Naomi grinned at him. "There's got to be some way to do this so that we avoid bodily injury. I don't want to start your head bleeding again."

"I'm all ears."

"Back up against that wall, and I'll lean against this one. Then we'll just wiggle down like this."

She demonstrated and he followed suit. It took some maneuvering, and he wasn't as good at the wiggling as she was. When they were finally seated cross-legged, their knees were touching, and they just about filled the space.

"Cozy," Dane commented as he glanced around. For the time being, he had to believe that the room provided a safe enough spot for them to talk. The lever had been cleverly concealed—he wouldn't have thought to even look for it. And he strongly doubted that Michael Davenport had. "What is this place?"

Naomi leaned forward, kept her voice low. "It's Hattie Haworth's secret room."

He raised a brow. "I'm a trained investigator. The minute you pulled the lever, I figured out the secret room thing. But why did she need one? And how did you find it?"

"When my sister Jillian first discovered the place, the whole tower was boarded up. Supposedly because Hattie haunted it. But a few boards and the rumors of a ghost didn't stop Jillian. She's always been a fools-rush-in-where-angels-fear-to-tread type. So she tore them down and decided that once the tower was rehabbed, it would make the perfect place for our new home. She was also the one who discovered this secret room."

"My brother Ian unearthed some rumors about Hattie haunting the place."

"Not just rumors. Hattie is definitely here."

"You've seen her?"

"Just the one time." She shared the details of the day

that Jillian had first brought them up to Hattie's room and what they'd seen for a moment as they'd stood, champagne glasses raised, looking into the mirror.

Dane nodded, thinking of the expression on Michael Davenport's face.

"You don't seem surprised or skeptical," Naomi observed.

"I think Davenport might have seen something just before he screamed. When I first opened the door to the tower, the place was as cold as a meat locker. After he hit me the first time, my back was to the mirror so he was facing it. He saw something, I'm certain of it. If he hadn't—well, just let's say that Hattie may have saved my life."

She reached out, placed a hand over one of his. "Then we definitely owe her one."

"Yeah." Dane glanced curiously around the small space again. "Do you have any idea what she used it for?"

Naomi studied him for a moment. "All we found in here was the hatbox." Lifting her tote off it, she revealed the box.

Dane studied it. "She used a secret room to hide a special hat?"

"No. There's no hat in there. Naomi lifted the box and positioned it between their crossed legs. "See for yourself."

Dane read the writing on the parchment.

Fantasy Box. Choose carefully. The one you select will come true.

Then, brows raised, he met Naomi's eyes.

"We think it might be a clue as to what kind of

business Hattie turned to once she established herself here at Haworth House. At the very least, it's an interesting insight into how she spent her leisure time."

Dane glanced down at the box again. "Ian didn't come up with even a whiff of anything like that. Did you choose one of the fantasies?"

"We all did."

He kept his eyes steady on hers. "What was yours?"

She lifted her chin. "I didn't even tell my sisters."

He said nothing.

Annoyance and a hint of defiance crept into her eyes. "I'll give you one guess."

He smiled slowly. "The most forbidden one of all—making love with a priest?"

"Yes. And once I drew that fantasy out, there didn't seem to be any escaping it. I think Hattie even left it in the hallway outside my door on the first night I was here."

"Only it turns out I'm not a priest. Lucky for us."

She folded her arms across her chest and frowned at him. "Lucky in what way?"

"We're going to have to talk about that." And they would. There were several things he wanted to talk to Naomi about.

For now, he set the hatbox aside and leaned forward to brush his lips across hers. He'd meant it to be a quick, friendly kiss. His intention changed the instant her mouth softened against his. This time it wasn't warmth he felt, but that sudden flash fire, that electric current in the blood that she'd brought to him from the first moment their eyes had met across that courtyard. Desire lanced through him.

Kissing her was a mistake. Her mouth was a fever. It was heaven. And it wasn't nearly enough. Dragging his lips from hers, he took them on a lightning-fast journey across her jaw, down her throat.

"I thought we talked…" She gasped. "I thought we had our priorities straight."

"Yeah." He nipped his way along her collarbone, then dug his fingers into her waist and dragged her closer. Their knees bumped, and he took an elbow to the ribs before she was finally straddling him.

"Too many clothes," she complained.

Yeah. He seconded that. He might have managed to express his agreement out loud if she hadn't been moving against him, center to center, heat to heat. The strength drained out of him as quickly as if she'd pulled a plug. Weakness swamped him. No woman had ever made him weak before.

As his brain cells clicked off, one by one, he was vaguely aware that she lifted herself to her knees, then into a squatting position. And all the time she wiggled out of her shorts and panties, her mouth stayed busy on his, her lips teasing, her teeth tormenting.

"I don't understand this. I can't seem to stop myself."

No problem. Once again, he was almost certain he hadn't managed to say the words aloud.

Even when she drew back for a moment to fumble with his zipper, he couldn't find the strength to lift his arms, to pull her back.

"Condom." He hoped he'd at least said that word

aloud, but he wasn't sure. He couldn't have heard it anyway above the hammering of his heart, the pounding of his blood. It wasn't until he felt her fingers sheathing him in protection that some of his strength finally flowed back into him.

He gripped her hips and lifted. She sank onto him, closed around him and tightened.

"Dane," she gasped his name. "I want you." Then her mouth sought his again.

"Take me."

He wasn't sure who said it, him or her. But he didn't have a choice. He let her rule with her desperation, her greed. He gloried in the sensations as her mouth singed his cheeks, her hands scorched his shoulders. And all the while her hips pumped and pumped and pumped.

He'd never known it was possible to want this much, to need this much—until he was sure that before she was through with him, he would shatter. And there was nothing to do to stop it. Helpless, totally hers, he felt himself arch.

Then she rode him until she reached her own release.

WHEN NAOMI FINALLY FOUND THE strength to open her eyes, she discovered that she was sitting on the floor next to Dane. And she had no clear idea how she'd gotten there. His arm was around her shoulder, their backs were against the same wall and their legs were stretched out toward the opposite wall. His reached. Hers didn't.

Angling her head so that she could see him, she noted that his eyes were still closed. As she studied his face in profile, she felt something tighten around her heart for just an instant before it went into free fall. The words he'd said on the balcony came back to her: *This is more than lust.*

And in spite of what they'd just done, which definitely had to have a high rating on the lust-o-meter, she was pretty sure he was right. A mix of emotions marched through her with panic in the lead, twirling a big baton.

Ruthlessly, she shoved them down. This was no time to sort through what she was feeling. This was not the time to have done what they'd just done!

"Are you all right?" she asked.

His lips curved as he opened his eyes and turned to face her. "Isn't that supposed to be my line?"

"Not this time. I think I just ravished you."

"Feel free to repeat the performance. Anytime."

She reached down to wiggle into the panties and shorts that were still looped around one of her ankles. "We didn't come in here for a ravishing. We came here to see if we could find over a hundred million dollars on a key ring I've been carrying around for two weeks."

"Right." He reached for her tote and handed it to her. "You can do the honors."

But she didn't reach into it right away. Instead, she said, "I don't understand what's happening between us."

"You will. When the time is right, you'll sort it out. We both will."

Not exactly the response she wanted. Something tightened around her heart again. What would she like him to say? That he was as uncertain and confused as she was? Perhaps. Or something glib and polished and reassuring—something that Michael would have said? Would she have preferred a lie? Because she couldn't or didn't want to deal with the questions right now, she reached into her tote, fished for the set of keys and pulled them out.

Dane took them and spread the key chain out in his hand. For a moment they studied it in silence.

To Naomi's way of thinking, it was ordinary enough in appearance. There was a little crystal heart and a sterling silver key dangling from a stainless steel chain. The ring that held the keys was ordinary enough, too— the kind that you had to twist your keys onto, breaking at least one nail and swearing several times in the process.

"Tell me exactly what happened the night he gave it to you at the Four Seasons," Dane said.

Naomi thought back to the evening that she'd relived in her mind numerous times. "It was a Tuesday so I worked until past seven. I'd walked five blocks toward home when Michael pulled over in a cab and stepped out on the curb."

"He didn't call?"

She shook her head, met his eyes. "No. He just pulled up. He apologized, said it was a spur-of-the-moment thing, but he'd wanted to see me. He asked me to go to the Four Seasons with him for a drink. I was tired. I might have begged off, but he was already drawing me toward the cab. He had a way about him that was very persuasive."

"Did he often do spur-of-the-moment things?" Dane asked.

Naomi's brow furrowed. "No. Michael liked to

plan everything. But I didn't think about it at the time because I was tired."

"But he would know your routine. You work late on Tuesdays."

She nodded. "What are you thinking?"

"Maybe he did plan it—but he didn't want to drop by the office or your apartment. He had to have known that his time was running out. What did you talk about in the cab?"

Naomi pressed fingers against her eyes. "Nothing much. My day—he asked about my day. I'd been working on a case with Thomas Fairchild and he'd been hovering, checking on me every hour or so. Then I asked Michael about his day. He said it had been one of those hectic ones when he'd looked forward to seeing me."

"How did Davenport seem? Tense? Out of sorts?"

"No. He seemed the same. Smooth. In control. That's the way he always was."

"And when you got to the Four Seasons?"

"He ordered champagne and then excused himself for a few minutes."

"What did you do while he was gone?"

Her brow furrowed again. "I pulled out one of my notebooks and jotted down some ideas I'd just come up with." She drew her notebooks out of her tote. "I always carry at least one of these because ideas about cases come to me at very inconvenient times. Sometimes even when I'm in court. That night I thought of something very important about the case I'd been working with Thomas."

Dane looked at the notebook. "You haven't used one while you've been here."

"No. I brought the tote and everything in it up here because I wanted to make a fresh start. I intended to buy a new notebook in Belle Bay today, but then I got distracted."

"How long before Davenport came back?"

"Five minutes, ten. He'd gone to the gift shop and bought the key chain as a memento of our first date at the Four Seasons."

"It sure looks like a gift shop purchase."

"He asked for my old key ring and then he insisted on taking my keys off it and twisting them onto the new one. It took a while. I excused myself and went to the ladies room while he was still working on it."

"What then?" Dane prompted.

"When I came back to the table, Michael was talking to Leo King and Thomas Fairchild. They'd stopped by with a client for a drink. When they left, Michael and I toasted with champagne and he told me that he had to go away for a while."

Reaching over, she picked up the chain by the sterling silver key and held it up. "He told me that he was giving me the key to his heart." In the stark light of the bulb overhead, the crystal heart gleamed. "I can't see anything about this key chain that might be worth over one hundred million dollars."

"I have to agree. Are you sure this is the one he gave you that night?"

She frowned down at it. "It has to be. I've had it either in my hand or in my tote ever since. Even during my first interview with the FBI when they went through everything, it never left my sight."

"And if it's been in this secret room almost since your arrival, Davenport couldn't have found it and made a switch yet."

Her eyes flew to his. "You think that was his plan?"

Dane sighed. "I'm still trying to figure out his plan. What we know is that he took you to the Four Seasons on the spur of the moment the night before he disappeared. Presumably to say goodbye. He also gave you a little souvenir. My gut still tells me he passed you the portable artifact for temporary safekeeping. Let's see what else you've got in that tote."

Twenty minutes later, they'd examined the other gifts Michael had given her and lined them up along the cramped floor space.

"Nothing." Naomi met Dane's eyes. "Every one of the things he gave me is exactly what it seems. What do we do next?"

One by one he loaded the mementos back into the bag. "We thought we'd figured it out. So now we have to back off and try to come at it from a different perspective." He took her hand and together they managed to make it to their feet. "First, we're going to let Sheriff Kirby know that Davenport is on the island and he's been in the hotel. Then we're going to find a place where we can talk that's a bit more accommodating than a secret room that was built to hold a hatbox and not much else. And we're going to get a second opinion on the Michael gifts. Maybe we missed something."

THE MORE ACCOMMODATING PLACE turned out to be Avery Cooper's suite of rooms above his office. She'd led Dane to the lobby first to find Avery. The stares they'd received from several of the guests gave her some clue as to how they must look, and the moment her friend had seen them, he'd hurried them into his office and then up the stairs to his suite.

Once Avery had gotten the *Reader's Digest* version of their earlier encounter with Michael Davenport, he'd taken over. By the time Nate Kirby had arrived, she and Dane had showered and changed into the fresh clothes that Avery had instructed the staff to gather from their respective rooms.

Sipping a glass of wine, Naomi leaned back against the counter in Avery's kitchen while he refilled a tray with sandwiches he'd ordered up from the kitchen. Through the door to the living room, she could see Dane and Nate using the tools Avery had also provided to disassemble the Michael gifts. The two men were currently working on a snow globe. When they'd begun, Avery had invited her to help him replenish their food, but so far, she hadn't had to do anything but watch.

She hadn't been of much use to Nate or Dane, either. So she'd reverted to her old habit of scribbling down notes and ideas. Once he'd noticed her using a paper napkin, Avery had provided her with a yellow legal pad.

Setting the sandwiches on the counter, Avery moved closer and pitched his voice low. "They both got the Bob the Builder gene. I didn't."

She flicked him a look. "Neither did I. And I like the genes you got."

He grinned at her and picked up his wine. "Me, too. Now, tell me about Dane MacFarland."

She looked at Dane, who was attacking the snow globe with a screwdriver while Nate supervised. And her heart took a little lurch. "He's not a priest."

"Yeah, I got that about three minutes after you got here tonight. I have to tell you I liked the priest persona, but the tough investigator thing has a lot going for it, too. And you're still interested in him."

It wasn't a question, so she didn't bother to deny it or even hedge. Instead, she set her glass down, paced away. "Yes, but…"

"But what?"

Turning back to face him, she raised her hands and then dropped them. "It's complicated."

Moving to her, Avery placed his hands on her shoulders. "Don't make it more complicated than it is, sugar. You're still hot for him. And it's mutual. Trust me. I can tell by the way you look at each other."

"The problem is I feel more than heat. Not that there isn't plenty of that. There is. But I think I might be falling in love with him."

The words, the fact that she'd spoken them aloud had fear snaking up her spine.

There was a beat of silence before Avery squeezed her shoulders and said in a matter-of-fact tone, "Well. Lucky for you, he's not a priest then, so he's available."

"I don't even know him. We talked at the beach and he told me some stuff about his background."

"I sincerely hope you did more than just talk."

Though she couldn't prevent her lips from twitching, she managed to say, "This isn't funny."

Avery drew her close for a hug. "Tell me."

She tipped her face back and met his eyes. "It's all happened so fast. I don't know how much of what he's told me is the truth and how much is something he made up to go with his cover story. I don't know anything about him."

She glanced past her friend's shoulder to see Dane upending the contents of the snow globe into a bowl.

Her heart took another lurch. How in the world had it come to this?

"He came here, lied to me, because he has a score to settle with Michael. I should hate him, but I don't. I want him more than I've wanted any other man. More than I've wanted anything except for my sisters to have a good life. But his primary goal is to get his man."

"So? You want to get that swine, too, don't you?"

She stared at him. "Of course. I also want to get the money back to the people he swindled."

"You know, Naomi. I'm one of those cockeyed optimists who believe that you can have your cake and eat it, too. First get *his* man, Michael Davenport, and then you go after *your* man." Grabbing the tray of sandwiches, Avery sailed past her. "Get a few more beers, will you?"

Naomi found herself staring at Avery's back for three full beats before she snatched up her legal pad, the beers and her wine. Her head was still spinning a bit as she took her place on the sofa that sprawled in a *U* around the coffee table. Nate had just finished loading the remains of Michael's gifts into her tote.

"There isn't anything in this pile of junk that's worth jack shit," he said.

"I agree," Dane said. "But I still believe that Davenport passed her something important that night at the Four Seasons. Otherwise, why bother to meet her there at all." He turned to her then. "What have you got in your notes, Naomi?"

Surprised, Naomi glanced down at the legal pad Avery had given her. "Scribbles mostly."

"I don't think so," Dane said. "The way you described it, your process is to jot down things when you want to make sure you remember something important."

That was true enough. She glanced at her notes. "I did most of this after you had me run through the sequence of events of that final evening for Nate. But it's just a time line. Thomas Fairchild spoke with me one last time as I left. Four or five blocks from the office, Michael had his cab pull over and pick me up. We went to the Four Seasons, Michael excused himself. And I thought of something to do with the case I was working on with Thomas, so I wrote it down. Michael came back with the key chain and started transferring my keys. I went to the ladies room, and when I came back Thomas and Leo were at our table chatting with Michael. Then Michael handed me his parting gift, paid the tab and he had the cab take me home."

"He didn't escort you in person to your apartment?" Dane asked. "I don't think I asked about that before."

"No. He had the doorman at the hotel hail a cab, but he didn't go with me. I assumed he took the next one."

"Was that like him—to just send you home?"

Naomi shook her head. "But he'd just told me he had to go away."

Nate looked at Dane. "He avoided her office and her apartment—places that he suspected or knew were already under surveillance."

"But he takes her to a public place where both of them could be seen," Dane said. "And in fact they *were* seen by Thomas Fairchild and Leo King."

Nate turned to Naomi. "Interesting that your two bosses, Davenport and you all happened to be at the Four Seasons the night when Davenport was singing you his swan song."

"And the same group is here at Haworth House right now," Avery pointed out.

Dane and Nate exchanged a look. "I don't much like coincidences," Nate said.

"I'm with you there," Dane replied.

Naomi stared at them. "You can't believe that Thomas and Leo are involved in this."

"It would explain why Davenport didn't try to snatch your purse in town this morning. Someone else beat him to it."

Naomi opened her mouth again, but whatever else she would have said was cut off by the shrill sound of an alarm.

Avery moved first, but the two men were on his heels as he pushed open the balcony doors. Even bringing up the rear, Naomi caught the tang of smoke in the air.

Avery whirled on them. "I hate to break up the party, but there's a fire in the hotel. I have to marshal the staff, get the hotel cleared."

With a glance at Dane, Nate said, "I'll go with you, Avery."

"Rooms on this side of the hotel evacuate to the gardens," Avery called over his shoulder. "Rooms on the other go out to the driveway."

When Dane's fingers closed around her arm, Naomi said, "I have to help. This is my hotel, my home."

"This could be a trap."

"You think Michael set a fire?"

"If I were Davenport, this is exactly what I'd do. I'd create a huge distraction. He hasn't gotten from you what he needs, and accomplishing that isn't proving to be the cakewalk he probably planned on taking. He's furious with you. And he believes in getting even."

"I still have to do what I can for the guests. Don't tell me you wouldn't do the same." Out of habit, she grabbed her tote off the coffee table as she started toward the door.

"Okay. All right. I'll come with you. Any problems, you do what I say."

14

FORTY-FIVE MINUTES LATER, Naomi stood with Dane at the far end of the garden. The darkened maze loomed to their left, and behind them, the sea crashed against the terraced rocks that bordered the hotel at the back. Guests had gathered in scattered groups along the lighted paths, waiting to return to their rooms.

"I'm so proud of Avery and the staff," she murmured.

"Avery's a good man," Dane commented.

They'd worked like a well-oiled machine, keeping the guests calm and moving as they'd evacuated the hotel. The fire engines from the village had arrived within the first fifteen minutes with a flourish of sirens and flashing lights. Right now staff members and firemen were checking the hotel room by room to find the source of the fire.

A few minutes ago, Nate had found them to let them know that much. Then she and Dane had wandered along the paths updating the guests. Since then a degree of normalcy had returned. Conversations picked up among the clusters of people. The smell of smoke had dissipated, replaced by the scent of hyacinths and roses. Hattie's tower pierced a lighter colored sky where stars pinwheeled brightly.

Naomi was about to will some of her tension away when she felt a prickling along the back of her neck. She glanced around quickly.

"What?" Dane asked.

"Just a feeling," she murmured. "I get it when someone's watching me."

Dane scanned the groups of guests and she followed the path of his gaze with her own. Everyone's attention seemed to be totally focused on the hotel. And except for the hedges of the maze, there was nowhere to hide.

She jumped when the bullhorn sounded, then relaxed as a voice announced, "All clear. You can reenter the hotel. All clear."

"Naomi?"

Hearing her name, she turned to see Leo King approaching.

"Are you all right?" he asked. "When I didn't see you at the front of the hotel, I circled back here."

"I'm fine." She smiled at Leo. "What about Thomas?"

"He's fine, probably moving back into the hotel right now. I told him I needed to check on you."

She felt Dane's hand tighten slightly on her arm, and she shot him a sideways glance.

"I'm Leo King." Leo extended his hand.

"Dane MacFarland." Dane released her arm to shake Leo's hand. At the moment of contact, his body jerked and Naomi gasped as he dropped to the ground.

Before she could get a sound past the fear in her throat, before she could even drop to her knees, a hand gripped her arm and she felt something hard jab into her side.

"He's all right," Leo said in a very soft voice. "I just stunned him. But this gun—" he jabbed her again "—has a silencer and it could prove lethal to both of you. Do you want me to shoot one of your guests to prove that I'm serious?"

"No." Naomi made herself focus. Dane was all right. For now. She and Leo were facing each other, the rocky terraces and the sea to their right. Out of the corner of her eye, she could see people moving back toward the hotel. The farther away they got, the better. How long before Dane came around? How long before Nate or Avery came to check on her? And put themselves in mortal danger.

"Leo, what are you doing? What do you want?"

He jabbed her again. "I want what's mine." The voice was Leo's voice, quiet, patient. But there was a look in his eyes Naomi had never seen before.

"I want that hundred million that Davenport is trying to cheat me out of. He never should have given it to you. I'm the one who warned him that the jig was up. I had informants at the FBI who told me they were planning on an arrest the next morning. He told me to come to the Four Seasons so that he could pass the money to me. He'd converted it all into a few rare stamps. I was going to take them and hold on to them until the coast was clear. Then he would get a buyer and we'd split the profits."

Naomi stared at him. As he'd spoken, the tone of his voice had gradually changed to match the fury in his eyes. "You were working with Davenport?"

"No." Leo spit out the word. "He was working for *me*. I gave him the clients, I sold him on the idea of romancing you so that the firm would have a scapegoat when our clients' money disappeared. I thought of everything. Everything. And then he gave the money to you—right there at the Four Seasons. Right in front of me."

"What did he give me, Leo?" The hundred-million-dollar question, she thought a bit giddily.

"He gave you the stamps. I was there, using Thomas and a client as cover, so that Michael could unobtrusively pass the stamps to me. But he never did. Instead, after you came back from the ladies' room, he paid the bill and took you away. By the time I was able to follow him, he was gone."

Stamps. Naomi's mind was racing. No wonder they hadn't found anything in the key chain. Where in the world had Michael stashed the stamps?

"I don't know what you want, Leo."

"I want your tote. They have to be in there. But you're never away from it. If it isn't on your shoulder, it's right at your feet. I couldn't find a way to search it before I had to fire you."

"Is that why you hired someone to steal my purse this morning?"

Ignoring the question, Leo continued, "You didn't have it with you when we had drinks in the courtyard. That gave me a bad moment or two. I was going to make you take me to it. But I'll just relieve you of it now."

The gun didn't move as Leo grabbed the straps and pulled the bag from her shoulder. Then in horror she watched as his body jerked, then crumpled the same way Dane's had.

Except it wasn't a stunner in the hand of the man now facing her. It was a large pistol with a silencer attached to it.

"If you scream, if you so much as move, you'll end up beside him on the ground," Michael said.

For a moment, there was a roaring in her ears. The instant she recognized it as panic, she shoved it away.

"Now pick up the tote and hand it to me."

As her mind raced, she let her body follow his orders, leaning down to take the straps from Leo's hand, then straightening. She didn't let herself look at the man who'd just been shot. She kept her eyes on Michael's.

"Good girl," he said with a smile as he took the tote and slung it over his shoulder.

Go, she thought. *You've got what you want. Now, just go.*

"You've caused me a great deal of difficulty," he said in the same tone of voice that he might have used to make some comment on the weather. "Your friend there, too."

She felt it then—just the slightest pressure against her shoe. Dane. He'd moved his foot. Later, she wondered if she would even have noticed if it weren't that all her senses were so aware of him. He was awake, and that made the whole situation worse. If Dane moved…

"I thought of ways to make you suffer, and my one regret will always be that I ran out of time. But if I shoot him first?" He glanced at her and smiled. "Yes, I think that will do it."

"Wait." She moved then, a step to the side so that her foot connected solidly with Dane's knee. And then, praying that Dane was listening, she spoke to both men. "Before you do anything rash, you should know that your rare stamps aren't in that tote."

She counted one beat of silence before Michael said, "You're lying."

"You know I'm not." She drew in a deep breath and

prayed that she was right. "You can already sense that the weight isn't right." If she could just distract him long enough for…what? If Dane made a move, Michael would shoot him. She was going to have to handle this herself. "Empty the tote. See for yourself."

As he tipped out the contents, Michael kept his gun hand steady on her. At least it wasn't pointed at Dane. A quick glance at the ground was all he needed.

"Where are they?"

They. It was just that one simple word that told Naomi just where Michael Davenport had hidden the rare stamps. Finally. And with the knowledge came the outline of a plan. She just had to persuade Michael to go along with it. Panic threatened again, but she ignored it. She'd found a way to convince a priest to make love with her. She was going to get Michael Davenport up to that tower room. The odds of taking him down were much better there.

Pressing her foot again into Dane's knee, she prayed that he was reading her signals. "I can take you to the notebooks, but there's a price."

"No. I'm done with demands. Tell me where they are and I'll only kill him. I'll let you go."

"Right. I'm not quite the complete fool you took me for, Michael."

"Maybe not."

She ignored the tightening in his voice. "Here's the way it is. The notebooks are in the tower in a secret room. I'm the only one who knows where that room is, and Dane here is your only bargaining chip. You're not going to shoot him."

"You want me to let him live."

"Yes. Thanks to Leo, he's out for the count. Besides, I know very well that you're still planning to kill me. I saw you shoot Leo King. But the only way to get your hands on those notebooks is to come with me to the tower." That would buy Dane some time. And once Michael was in the tower, maybe she could count on Hattie to help.

There was a beat of silence as Michael flicked a glance at the tower. "If you're lying…"

"There's only one way to find out. Unless you can't go back there."

"Of course, I can go back there." Carefully lowering the gun, he tucked it into his waistband beneath his shirt. Then he took her hand. "If you try anything—even so much as look at anyone the wrong way—I'll cut my losses, but I'll shoot a few of your guests before I make my escape."

Together, they started toward the hotel.

FEAR HELPED DANE CLEAR THE remaining fog from his mind. Hearing Michael Davenport's voice had jump-started his brain, but his body was still giving him trouble. When he'd moved a foot to let Naomi know that he was regaining consciousness, that was all he'd been able to move.

But she'd gotten his signal. And she deserved kudos for managing to fill him in on what she planned to do.

There was nothing wrong with Naomi Brightman's brain. One part of him admired the plan because it bought her some time. Another part of him was scared shitless.

She was taking Davenport up to that tower room, where she'd have to deal with both the man's greed and his gun—and an unpredictable ghost in the mix.

He made it to his knees and fought off a wave of dizziness. By the time he staggered to his feet, Nate joined him. The sheriff glanced down at the body. "Do I want to know about this right now?"

"It's Davenport's work. C'mon. I'll fill in the details as we go. The big picture is Naomi figured out the stamps are in her notebooks and she's taking Davenport to them. He'll kill her once he has his hands on them."

NAOMI TRIED TO IGNORE the buzzing sound in her ear as she and Michael joined the line of guests who were now moving back into the hotel. She had to get him away from Dane. If she could just get Michael past all the people he could hurt to the tower... Walking as quickly as she could, she forged an unobtrusive path through the crowd to the stairwell then started up the stairs.

"Good girl," Michael murmured as they passed the first landing. "So far, so good." When they began ascending the stone staircase to the first level of the tower, she felt the hard press of the gun in her side once again. And he made sure she felt it again when they reached the oak door to Hattie's tower.

"No tricks. I won't be buying in to them this time."

Somehow she kept her hand steady as she fished out the key and turned it in the lock. Dane was coming. It was that thought, that certainty, that had panic tightening inside of her. He'd waste no time in following her. She had to get Michael into the tower room first. Then she had to find a way to distract him.

"No tricks," she promised as she pulled the door open. But the sudden rush of cold air gave her hope that Hattie might be up to a few.

"What have you got—some kind of super air-conditioning in this place?"

Naomi flipped a switch, and the stairwell was flooded with light. Then she started up the stairs. She sensed the hesitation behind her. *Not yet, Hattie.* She sent the thought spiraling upward. "Coming?"

As they climbed the circular stairs together, Michael's breathing became more labored.

Waiting until they'd both stepped into the tower room, she said, "This room was the one Hattie Haworth used as a bedroom. Do you know anything about her?"

"Yeah." Michael flicked a glance around the room. "She was a washed-up movie star who came here and turned herself into a hermit. Greta Garbo with none of the glamour."

The beveled mirror was out of her sight line, but she caught the flash all the same. Hope and the connection she'd always felt with Hattie helped her, but Naomi knew that the spirit of the dead ex-movie star wasn't the whole answer. And she could sense that Dane was getting closer. *Stall.* She had to stall and keep Michael distracted.

If he were on one of her juries, she'd know what approach to take. Turning, she faced him and suddenly it came to her. Ego. "Will you just tell me one thing, Michael? How did you manage to hide the stamps in one of my notebooks without my knowing?"

"Easy. I did it that night at the Four Seasons. When you went to the ladies' room, you left the notebook on the table."

She had, she recalled. She'd gotten it out to jot some notes while he'd been gone for those few moments. "What if I hadn't gone to the restroom?"

He smiled then. "I would have suggested that you needed to powder your nose."

The confidence in his tone had her spine stiffening.

"You would have gone. You're very…malleable."

Not anymore. But she didn't say the words aloud. Behind him, she could see just the top of Dane's head appear on the spiral staircase.

Knowing she had to keep Michael focused on her, she said, "Hattie's still here, you know. She haunts the tower."

"You're not going to scare me with a ghost."

The air trembled.

Michael's gun hand didn't. He stepped forward and jabbed the gun into her. "I won't kill you with the first shot. Before I'm done, you'll beg me to let you show me the secret room."

Slowly, she backed to the wall, felt for the lever and pulled it. Though she didn't spare them a glance, she knew the notebooks were there on the floor just where she'd left them. And she knew the instant that Michael spotted them. If he would just step into the room, she would shut the door and trap him….

But Michael didn't go into the room. Instead, he met her eyes. "Good girl. Now, I'll give you your reward. One quick shot. You'll barely feel it."

"Do that and you die."

Dane.

In a lightning fast move, Michael's arm went around her neck, and he jerked her in front of him as he whirled. Before fear could register, she felt the hard press of the gun against her temple.

"Wrong," Michael said. "You're the one who'll—"

The sentence ended on a choked sound as Hattie Haworth materialized in front of them.

"You—" Michael said. "You're not real."

But Naomi felt his heart race against her back as the image grew stronger, and light flashed brightly in the beveled mirror.

Hattie was just as Naomi remembered her—the long tumble of red gold curls, the flowing dress that didn't quite touch the floor. But she wasn't in the mirror this time.

As she drifted toward them, hysteria tinged Michael's voice. "Stop! Stop or I'll shoot."

The problem was that Hattie had positioned herself in front of Dane as if she were trying to protect him. But Naomi was pretty sure that a ghost couldn't take a bullet.

When Michael's gun arm swung toward Hattie, Dane sprang forward.

"No." Fueled by both adrenaline and fear, Naomi flung herself on Michael's gun arm. The shot made barely a sound, but she felt the heat of the bullet. Off balance, she stumbled and landed on the floor just in time to see Dane tackle Michael. And he'd lunged right through Hattie to do it.

Both men crashed into the wall, then rolled across the floor, first one on top and then the other. As Dane gained the upper position and pounded a fist into Michael's face, Nate reached the top of the stairs. "Hey, MacFarland, save me a turn."

But Michael was no longer moving.

Naomi's head spun as Hattie's image began to fade. Before it disappeared completely, Naomi was almost sure it winked at her. She tried to shake the dizzy feeling out of her head, but it wouldn't go.

"Are you all right?"

The moment Dane's hands closed around her upper arm, she gasped and her vision began to gray.

"Dammit, Naomi. He shot you. You're bleeding."

She saw the proof of that on Dane's hands before her world went black.

EASING HER LEGS OVER THE SIDE of her bed, Naomi said, "I want to get dressed." By her rather hazy calculations, she'd been in bed for over a day and a half.

"You're still several short of the forty-eight hours of bed rest the doctor ordered," Reese said.

"And you always insisted that we follow doctor's orders," Jillian added. "Payback time."

"Besides, we just got here this morning." Reese yawned. "If you get dressed, then we'll have to change clothes, and I'm still suffering from jet lag."

Naomi frowned at Reese. Since her youngest sister seldom wore anything but jeans and a T-shirt under her chef's jacket, she didn't see that changing clothes would be an exhausting process. But she didn't say that.

"Besides, we have something we want to talk to you about," Jillian said.

They were trying to distract her, and it was a strategy she was very familiar with.

For a second the images of those last few moments in the tower room flashed into her mind just as they had each time she'd drifted into sleep. She experienced once again the tightening of Michael's arm around her throat and the fear and desperation she'd felt as he'd swung his gun arm toward Dane. But in the fitful dreams she'd had ever since she'd been sedated, the bullet always flew through Hattie and found its target. Dane had fallen to the ground and blood had blossomed on his shirt.

Ruthlessly she pushed the picture away. She had a goal here. She wanted to see Dane. He hadn't visited her. At least she couldn't remember that he had.

"I don't think that young man who stitched me up was a real doctor. You didn't see him. He looked like he was twelve." But she didn't push to her feet. For one thing, Reese had propped her own feet on the side of the bed so that Naomi would have had to climb over them to get to the closet. For another, she still had enough pain meds in her system to make her reevaluate the effort it would take to actually select clothes and put them on. The sneaky little health practitioner had knocked her out for hours—long enough for her sisters to fly in from California and Europe. Too long.

Reese rolled her eyes at Jillian. "I can't imagine that the doc wasn't fully credentialed. The FBI flew him in from the mainland. He wouldn't have gotten past your private army if he wasn't the real McCoy."

"My private army?"

"Avery, the hunky sheriff and the even hunkier Dane MacFarland," Jillian said. "They've been vetting anyone who wants to see you. So far we're the only two they've permitted in. They've refused entry to some pretty intimidating guys in suits."

Naomi closed her eyes. "Probably the FBI."

"Don't worry about it. Dane is filling them in on everything that happened," Reese said. "He even hit the high points with us."

"The hundred million dollars' worth of stamps were glued between the pages in one of your notebooks, Michael Davenport is in custody, and his unlucky partner—

your old boss, Leo King—is dead. And Dane says that you may have saved his life."

"I didn't. It was just that I didn't think Hattie could stop a bullet. It was going to go right through her and—" She trailed off to block the images that threatened to flood her mind again.

"I'm not sure that your trio of protectors has reported the role that Hattie played in all of this to the suits." Reese waved a lazy hand. "Of course, if you suddenly get dressed and go down to the lobby, you can fill them in on the preternatural side of the case. They'll probably keep running you through it for hours."

"Okay, okay." Naomi inched her way back to lean against her pillows.

"You really did see Hattie again?" Jillian asked.

Naomi nodded. "I swear she winked at me."

"I don't want to hear about Hattie," Reese said. "She's old news. I want to know about Dane MacFarland. Who is he?"

Naomi pressed a hand against her heart to still the quick thud. She wanted the answer to that question even more than they did. Just who was Dane MacFarland?

"Well?" Jillian prompted.

Naomi raised her hands and dropped them. "That's just it. I don't know who he is."

Shooting an I-told-you-so glance at Reese, Jillian sat down on the foot of the bed and crossed her legs. "Avery said the two of you may have something serious going on."

"What else did he tell you?" Naomi asked.

"That's it. Then he locked up his lips and threw away the key." Reese pantomimed the gesture. "He just didn't want us to be operating totally in the dark."

"While you were still weaving in and out of the meds,

we talked to Dane for a bit." Jillian exchanged a look with Reese. "Just a little sisterly cross-examination. He told us he came to the island masquerading as a priest to catch Michael Davenport."

Naomi frowned. Evidently the man had time to talk to everyone but her.

"Well?" Jillian prompted again.

The look in Reese's eyes was equally expectant. "We need the details. All of them."

Resigned, Naomi leaned back against her pillows and gave up the story.

DANE HEARD THE LAUGHTER in the room when he and Avery stood outside the door to knock. It should have eased his nerves. It didn't.

When someone called out, "Come in," Avery led the way and they found three women sitting in a circle on the bed.

The instant he saw Naomi, a rush of emotions hit him again like a sucker punch to the belly.

She was fine. He hadn't lost her. Those were the words he'd repeated over and over again while he and Nate had fashioned a tourniquet to stop the bleeding. And they'd become a chant in the back of his mind in the long hours since as he'd waited for the doctor's prognosis and dealt with the details of wrapping the Michael Davenport case up.

The fear that had been rolling around inside of Dane since he'd stepped into the tower room and seen Davenport's gun pressed against her temple only faded now as he saw her sitting up—alive.

Then his heart didn't just take a tumble. It went into freefall. He loved her. He wasn't sure when it had happened or quite how. And dammit, he couldn't quite feel his knees.

When three pairs of eyes locked with his, he managed to say, "Naomi…" Then he completely lost his train of thought.

It was Jillian who rose first and ushered everyone out of the room, leaving a deafening silence behind.

"You brought flowers," Naomi finally said.

Dane glanced down at the bunch of roses he held, then back at Naomi. "Right. Avery's idea."

And she didn't look happy to see them.

"I picked them from the gardens. Avery said it would be all right." Then because he wasn't sure what else to do, he set them on the foot of the bed. He'd come up here with a plan. The flowers were a part of it.

"Naomi."

"Dane."

They spoke at the same time, then Naomi said, "You first."

"I like your sisters," he said, stalling. He wanted to touch her but if he did, he knew the plan—whatever it had originally been—would change. So he stuffed his hands in his pockets.

Silence thundered between them again.

"Look," Naomi said. "I know why you brought the flowers."

Good, he thought. At least one of them did.

"You're trying to say goodbye."

"No." The sudden jolt her words gave him shocked him from his daze. "No." He moved around the foot of the bed and sat down next to her. As much as he wanted to, he still didn't touch her.

"I brought the flowers because I want to start over with you. No." He ran a hand through his hair. "That's not it. I want to persuade you to start over with me. Clean slate."

She folded her hands tightly together in her lap and studied him in that solemn way of hers.

Her silence triggered a new wave of panic.

"Start over," she finally said.

"Yes." He rose, paced away, then walked back. "I... had some time to think." The seemingly endless hours when he'd been waiting for the young doctor's prognosis and then while she was sleeping off the meds. "I talked to your sisters, and it occurred to me that we got off to a bad start. I told a lot of lies. I'm sorry for that."

He moved closer to the bed, but he didn't dare sit down.

"I want to give you time to get to know me. We can take things as slowly as you want."

She studied him for another long moment. "Do you really have a brother named Ian?"

He winced. "Yes."

"And what you told me when we were on the beach about the cop who raised you and the brother and sister you haven't been able to locate yet?"

"All of that was true. I told you things I've never even shared with Ian. I couldn't understand it."

He moved to the bed and sat down. "But I do now. I told you all of that because even then I was falling in love with you."

The shock in her eyes had fear gripping him with rusty claws.

"You don't know me," she said.

He grabbed her hands, held tight. "Yes, I do. That's just it, I know everything about you. Ian's good at research. I even know what brand of toothpaste you use. I knew about those notebooks, that you carried them with you everywhere. I should have figured out sooner that Davenport would have used them. I could have stopped—" He broke off as he glanced at the bandage on her arm.

Then he drew in a deep breath and let it out. "From now on, Naomi, I'll be honest with you. No more lies. The only thing that I didn't know about you when I decided to pose as Father MacFarland was the fact that when you were fourteen, you fell in love with a young priest."

He met her eyes. "If I had, I hope that I wouldn't have decided to masquerade as one. But I might have. I was pretty much willing to do anything, to use anyone to catch Davenport."

Naomi met his eyes steadily. She might not know everything about him, but she knew some important things. He loved his family. He was basically an honest man. A courageous one. And an understanding one. Someone she could depend on. It had helped to discover that his brother Ian was real and that what he'd told her on the beach was the truth.

But even barring those details, she knew him all right. Hadn't she recognized him on some level the first time she'd seen him?

Wasn't that why she was so afraid? "I don't want to start over," she said.

He grabbed her hands then, held on. "I'm not taking no for an answer here, Naomi."

She lifted her chin. "You've had your say. The least you can do is hear me out."

He didn't release her, but he nodded.

"I don't want to start over with you. I want to build on what we've already begun. And I have a confession to make."

His hands tightened painfully on hers. "What?"

"I'm falling in love with you, too. In fact, I think I already have."

He lifted her hands, pressed his lips to them. "We'll take things slowly this time, Naomi."

She pulled him closer, brushed her lips over his. "No, I don't think so. Why mess with success?"

As she deepened the kiss, she drew him down on top of her, and her hands became busy with the snap on his jeans.

"We can't...your arm..."

"We can...." She'd already freed him, and in spite of his words, his hands had made quick work of her panties.

"We'll just have to improvise." Her laugh was low, sultry, and held a future of promises.

With a groan, he tested her. She was so wet, so hot, so ready. His. As he slipped fully into her, he framed her face with his hands. "I never looked for this. Never expected to find someone...someone I don't want to live without. We're going to be improvising for the rest of our lives."

"That's the idea."

They were both smiling as he brought his mouth back to hers.

* * * * *

*Jillian's turn is next! Find out what secret
and forbidden fantasy she drew out
of Hattie's box next month in
TAKEN BEYOND TEMPTATION.*

Harlequin offers a romance for every mood!
See below for a sneak peek from our
suspense romance line
Silhouette® Romantic Suspense.
Introducing HER HERO IN HIDING by
New York Times bestselling author Rachel Lee.

Kay Young returned to woozy consciousness to find that she was lying on a soft sofa beneath a heap of quilts near a cheerfully burning fire. When she tried to move, however, everything hurt, and she groaned.

At once she heard a sound, then a stranger with a hard, harsh face was squatting beside her. "Shh," he said softly. "You're safe here. I promise."

"I have to go," she said weakly, struggling against pain. "He'll find me. He can't find me."

"Easy, lady," he said quietly. "You're hurt. No one's going to find you here."

"He will," she said desperately, terror clutching at her insides. "He always finds me!"

"Easy," he said again. "There's a blizzard outside. No one's getting here tonight, not even the doctor. I know, because I tried."

"Doctor? I don't need a doctor! I've got to get away."

"There's nowhere to go tonight," he said levelly. "And if I thought you could stand, I'd take you to a window and show you."

But even as she tried once more to pull away the quilts, she remembered something else: this man had been gentle when he'd found her beside the road, even when she had kicked and clawed. He hadn't hurt her.

Terror receded just a bit. She looked at him and detected signs of true concern there.

The terror eased another notch and she let her head sag on the pillow. "He always finds me," she whispered.

"Not here. Not tonight. That much I can guarantee."

Will Kay's mysterious rescuer protect
her from her worst fears?
Find out in HER HERO IN HIDING by
New York Times *bestselling author Rachel Lee.*
Available June 2010, only from
Silhouette® Romantic Suspense.

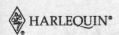
HARLEQUIN®

Showcase

Vicki Lewis Thompson

On sale May 11, 2010

Reader favorites from the most talented voices in romance

Save $1.00 on the purchase of 1 or more Harlequin® Showcase books.

SAVE $1.00 on the purchase of 1 or more Harlequin® Showcase books.

Coupon expires Oct 31, 2010. Redeemable at participating retail outlets.
Limit one coupon per purchase. Valid in the U.S.A. and Canada only.

Canadian Retailers: Harlequin Enterprises Limited will pay the face value of this coupon plus 10.25¢ if submitted by customer for this product only. Any other use constitutes fraud. Coupon is nonassignable. Void if taxed, prohibited or restricted by law. Consumer must pay any government taxes. Void if copied. Nielsen Clearing House ("NCH") customers submit coupons and proof of sales to Harlequin Enterprises Limited, P.O. Box 3000, Saint John, NB E2L 4L3, Canada. Non-NCH retailer—for reimbursement submit coupons and proof of sales directly to Harlequin Enterprises Limited, Retail Marketing Department, 225 Duncan Mill Rd., Don Mills, ON M3B 3K9, Canada.

52609015

U.S. Retailers: Harlequin Enterprises Limited will pay the face value of this coupon plus 8¢ if submitted by customer for this product only. Any other use constitutes fraud. Coupon is nonassignable. Void if taxed, prohibited or restricted by law. Consumer must pay any government taxes. Void if copied. For reimbursement submit coupons and proof of sales directly to Harlequin Enterprises Limited, P.O. Box 880478, El Paso, TX 88588-0478, U.S.A. Cash value 1/100 cents.

5 65373 00076 2   (8100)0 11651

HSCCOUP0410

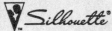

HARLEQUIN® *Romance*®

GIRLS' Weekend in VEGAS

Four friends, four dream weddings!

On a girly weekend in Las Vegas, best friends Alex, Molly, Serena and Jayne are supposed to just have fun and forget men, but they end up meeting their perfect matches! Will the love they find in Vegas stay in Vegas?

Find out in this sassy, fun and wildly romantic miniseries all about love and friendship!

Love Inspired

Bestselling author

JILLIAN HART

brings you another heartwarming story
from

the
GRANGER FAMILY RANCH

Rancher Justin Granger hasn't seen his high school sweetheart
since she rode out of town with his heart. Now she's back, with
sadness in her eyes, seeking a job as his cook and housekeeper.
He agrees but is determined to avoid her...until he discovers
that her big dream has always been him!

The Rancher's Promise

*Available June
wherever books are sold.*

Steeple
Hill®
LI87601

REQUEST YOUR FREE BOOKS!

2 FREE NOVELS PLUS 2 FREE GIFTS!

HARLEQUIN®

Blaze™

Red-hot reads!

HARLEQUIN® *Blaze*™

is proud to present

New York Times bestselling author

Vicki Lewis Thompson

with a brand-new trilogy,
SONS OF CHANCE
where three sexy brothers
meet three irresistible women.

Look for the first book
WANTED!

*Available beginning in June 2010
wherever books are sold.*

---

red-hot reads

www.eHarlequin.com

HB79548